Hidden Feelings Revealed

IS THERE MORE

ROYCE DIXON SR.

CONTENTS

PROLOGUE

I never imagined I would find myself in this situation. Losing my dad at such a young age was devastating, but to then lose my mother and my girlfriend within weeks of each other was almost unbearable. While I couldn't do anything to prevent my mom's passing, losing Jasmine was entirely my fault for failing to express my feelings. It's absurd when I think about it. As an attorney, communication is supposed to be my forte. I literally make a living by using my words every day, yet when it came to Jasmine, I chose not to. Now I find myself alone, surrounded by all the material possessions I could ever want, but none of it brings me joy or fills the void in my heart and life. How did I end up here? How did that young boy from the tough neighborhood, who always yearned for a family, transform into this? A successful businessman with his own law firm, earning a six-figure income, owning a house, and having the freedom to do whatever and go wherever he pleases. Despite all these accomplishments, I am here, sitting alone and unhappy, realizing that none of it truly matters. So, what do I do now? I can choose to wallow in self-pity and let life pass me by, or I can commit to therapy and rediscover the joy of living life to the fullest—the way my mother would have wanted me to.

HIDDEN

FEELING LIKE ME AGAIN

The phone rings:

"Hey, what up Frat? This is Mike." "Oh, what's up bruh?"

"Nothing much; I was m the neighborhood and wanted to stop by and check on you, if that's ok."

"Yea, I'm not doing anything; just watching the game. Come on through."

"Cool, I'll be there in about twenty minutes." Troy hears a car and looks out the window. Mike is walking to the door. Troy unlocks the door and they greet each other with their fraternity handshake. Mike says, "Man, what's up? I haven't seen or heard from you since your mom's funeral. How have you been?"

"To be honest Mike, I don't even know where to begin. When I tell you it's been rough—it's been rough for me these last four or five months. I have never been through anything like this in my life. Between my mom passing and the breakup with Jasmine, this has been the hardest time of my life. Oh, and check this out: I ran into her at the park not too long ago and she told me that while we were together, she had a one-night stand."

"What?!"

"Yea, that is what I said to myself; I couldn't believe it. She told me it was during the time when I was quiet and distant. We were just living in the same house as roommates."

"Bruh," Mike asks, "But you were living together as boyfriend and girlfriend, right?"

Troy says, "Yes, we were in theory, but not really. She kept trying to get me to talk and be present in the relationship, and for whatever reason I had checked out. I was just going through the motions of being her boyfriend. Oh! now…this will really trip you out. She had a kid, bro!"

"Are you serious?" Mike exclaims.

"Bro, I am so serious. I guess the guy she had the one-night stand with got her pregnant. She claims that's the reason she left the way that she did—she didn't know how to tell me. I can't front, that hurt a lot when she said it, and of course I played it off like it was no big deal…but man, that was like a knife in the heart. I have always wanted a kid, and Jasmine would have been a great mother. Then to hear her say that she had a kid with a random guy—ouch! I have been trying to deal with all that pain and heartache; that's why I have kept to myself all this time and no one has heard from me. I needed time to think about my life. I had to look in the mirror and see why it was so hard for me to talk about my hidden feelings and share them with anyone."

"How are you dealing with all this now?" Mike asks.

"Well, I have been talking to my new pastor a lot lately, and he has been counseling me and helping me through it. I'm also getting some professional help. I realize now that I have had issues that I have never been able to deal with, going all the way back to when my dad passed. Growing up without a man in the house—or really in my life—to show me how a man deals with his feelings or emotions really impacted me. Since I didn't have anyone to show me those things, I looked to the stereotypical men to teach me what it was like to be a man. Back in the day, my mom used to work a lot; so when I was a kid, I didn't have to talk about how I felt about things when I got mad or frustrated—I just dealt with it or buried it inside. Playing sports was another way that I would use as a way of dealing with my feelings; that was my outlet or stress reliever."

"Do you think that the counseling sessions have helped you at all?"

"Yea, I do," Troy replies.

"It opened my mind and helped me to think about some things—and it helped me to see myself."

"Wow, Frat! I had no idea that you had so much going on; had I known, I would have called or come through. You should have said something."

"I know, bruh," says Troy. "That's part of my problem—I have to remember that it's ok to talk about how I'm feeling or what's going on with me."

"Yea, most men have that problem, and for some strange reason, men just shut down when it comes to dealing with their emotions or feelings."

"What I'm seeing now is that we as men spend so much time playing the macho role, that we forget that it's ok to be a man that shares his feelings with others. In one of my sessions with the pastor, we talked about that and how we as men need to learn how to differentiate our feelings. For example, joy and happiness—are two separate feelings; two different emotions that feel similar, and yet are two different things. Another one that we have a habit of lumping together is love and lust," Troy says.

"Yea, we do miss the mark with that one, Troy."

"Before all of this happened to me, I never took the time to ask myself why. Why didn't my past relationships work? Why didn't I allow women to get close to me other than my mom? Now that I have been looking in the mirror, I see things a lot differently. I never wanted to know why, because it would force me to do just what I ended up doing: looking in the mirror. It would also force me to look at the whole situation and not just with what I was comfortable with. I'm learning that our past and our memories can bind us, keeping us from moving forward if they are not dealt with, because they can carry a form of pain that we have associated with that memory; and nine times out of ten we would rather not deal with them if we can—we will avoid it like the plague if we could. Mike, I would have never believed that this would be me. It makes sense, though; why I had to be in control and why me and Jasmine didn't work; why I have treated women the way I have and why I don't trust many people. At the end of the day, my happiness is on me, and I need to release all those old memories and past hurts and move forward."

"Well, bruh, it sounds like you're doing ok. I need to take off, Troy. If you need me, I'm here."

"I know Mike; and I appreciate you, my brother. Thanks for stopping by to check on me. It was good to see you."

"Same here."

A NEW CHAPTER BEGINS

Monday morning comes, and Terrance and Troy meet in the parking lot of their office. "Hey, what's up, Troy? I didn't know if you were coming in today."

"Yea I know, T; it's time for me to get back into the swing of things and move on with my life. I want to thank you for holding down the office while I was gone. I know you had your hands full with all my cases on top of all your cases—it's good to know that I have a partner that has my back. Better yet, a brother who has my back."

The two embrace and head into their offices, where both of their secretaries hand them their morning paper, messages, and court schedules for the day. After going through his messages, Troy heads into Terrance's office.

"Hey, do you want to head over to court together, and you can catch me up on the cases that we have?" Troy asks.

"Yea, that's fine. I'm done here, so I'm ready if you are."

A NEW DAY

"All rise, please. Court is now in session; the honorable Judge Anthony Walker presiding."

"Please be seated clerk. You may call the first case."

"Number one on the docket—case number 2022CF4237. The people of the state of Illinois versus Patricia Henderson. How does this case come before the court?"

Good morning; State Attorney Rashad Jones for the people."

"Good morning, your honor; Attorney Troy Brooks for the defendant Patricia Henderson. This case comes before you for arraignment. Your honor, Ms. Henderson would like to plead not guilty. We would waive the reading of rights of penalties, and ask that this case be set over until May 15th at 9 a.m."

"State, is this your agreement?" "Yes, your honor, it is."

"Ok, so ordered. This case is set on the docket for May 15th at 9 a.m. Next case."

"Officer, can you place Ms. Henderson in a conference room so that I may speak with her please?"

"Hello, Ms. Henderson, my name is Troy Brooks and I'm from the Law Offices of Brooks and Mays. Your cousin, Marla, has hired us to be your legal counsel."

"Oh, ok. I thought you were a public defender or something."

"No, not at all. I will be your private counsel. Now, Ms. Henderson, I need to ask you a couple of questions to get familiar with your case. Can you tell me what happened on the night in question?"

"He attacked me, and I killed him—as simple as that!"

"Well, what made him attack you? This was a sitting United States senator we are talking about. And how did you know him?" Troy asks.

"It doesn't matter why he attacked me or how I knew him— he attacked me, and I fought back. It's as simple as that; it was self-defense. Now your job is to get me off! That's all you need to know." As she slams her fist on the table and points her finger towards Troy.

"Ms. Henderson, it's not that simple. When you got arrested, you had the murder weapon in your trunk. I need to build a case and tell your story; I can't tell a jury that a senator just attacked you for no reason—I need more."

"Well, that's what happened! So, get me out of here—my baby girl needs me to be home with her. If nothing else, get me a reasonable bail amount so I can post bail and get home to my daughter."

"Alright, I'll file a motion for a bail reduction to at least get you out of custody for now. I'll be in touch."

Troy gets out his cell phone and calls Terrance.

"Hey, what's your afternoon looking like? I need to talk to you about this murder case. The victim is a sitting U.S. senator, and the defendant is hiding something. She is refusing to tell me anything other than it was self-defense. I don't see a motive and she won't tell me how they knew each other. We have our hands full here."

Terrance replies, "Well, I'm free. We can meet back at the office and try to come up with a strategy on how we are going to win this case—not to mention how we will manage the media coverage."

"Ok, well, I'll see you soon."

THAT ONE CO-WORKER

"Jasmine, could you please step into my office? I have something that I need to discuss with you."

"Sure, what's going on, Matt?"

"Jasmine, you know how we had discussed you overseeing Senator Johnson's murder case. Well, it looks like we are going to have to rethink things. Attorney Troy Brooks just entered his appearance on behalf of the defendant, and we don't want people to think that there is any type of bias or any conflict of interest in this case—this is going to be a media frenzy as it is. So, I think it's best that you sit this one out. I know how you were looking forward to prosecuting this case, being one of our best prosecutors."

"I understand what you're saying, Matt; however, me and Troy haven't been together for quite some time, and I can assure you that our relationship is over. I will do my job." Jasmine replies.

"I know you will, Jasmine; however, look at it from my point of view: if the media ever found out that you and Troy used to be an item and he won the case? People would say all kinds of crazy things and suggest that you threw the case or didn't fight as hard to win because you still had feelings for Mr. Brooks. You understand what I'm saying?" Matt asks.

"Yes, Matt, I do understand. It's just that this could be that case that prepares me for the next step when you retire."

"Jasmine, you're young and you're an incredibly talented prosecutor—your time will come, trust me. Look at what you have done already and how fast you have moved up. You're now the chief of the criminal division and your conviction rate is off the charts. We see the outstanding work that you have put in. It's one case, and we could still use your help with trying this case—you just won't be the lead attorney on this."

"Ok I get it! If you don't mind me asking: who is this case assigned to? Please don't say Alvin! I can already tell by that look that it's Alvin, isn't it?"

"Well, he is the deputy state's attorney.

"I know, I know; and you also know how he does everything he can to make me look bad because I got the promotion over him, and now his ego is hurt," Jasmine stated.

"I understand all that, Jasmine; I do. Alvin is a good prosecutor, though, and we need our best people on this case. I need you to be on board with this. Now, can you do this, or did I promote the wrong person? If I had my choice, you would be the one. I just can't. We can't let our personal life interfere, and the mayor will be watching us very closely since this is an election year. Now, can I count on you to help Alvin and me?" Matt asks.

"Yes, you have my word. I'll help him as much as I can."

"Good—I knew I had made the right decision."

Just then, there is a knock on the door. "Come in," Matt yells from behind his desk.

"It's Alvin. Um, you wanted to see me?"

"Yes, I did; come in and have a seat. Alvin, due to a conflict of interest between Jasmine and Mr. Brooks—who is now counsel for Patricia Henderson, the defendant in Senator Johnson's murder case—you will now become the lead prosecutor on this case, and Jasmine will assist you in any way that she can. I can't stress to you enough how important this case is with this being an election year and how much media attention this case is going to have. Do you have any questions? This case is scheduled for a bond hearing on May 15th at 9 a.m. in courtroom one for a bond reduction."

"Well, sir, I'll be ready. I will start getting up to speed on this case at once. Is that it, Matt?" asks Alvin.

"Yes, that's it Alvin; you and Jasmine better get to work."

As they both get up and walk out the door, Alvin heads towards his office and Jasmine towards hers. Alvin mutters under his breath, "I really don't need a babysitter." Jasmine hears him and understands that this may not be the best time for a conflict, so she goes back to her office.

Troy is now back at work and looking for Terrance; he finds him in the conference room talking with a client.

"Um, excuse me, Terrance—when you're done, could you please stop by my office? I have something that I need to talk to you about."

"No problem, Troy. Mr. Burton and I, are just about done here."

"Hey, what's up? You wanted to talk? I just got back from court. Have you heard anything about Senator Johnson's murder case?"

"Like I was saying over the phone, Ms. Henderson is not talking—the only thing she will say is that it was self-defense. She wouldn't even tell me how they knew each other or how they came to be in the same room with each other."

"I wish I could help, Troy. All I know is that her cousin, Marla Bordeaux, came into the office, paid our retainer, and gave us the court date. Other than that, we are shooting in the dark." Terrance says.

"Well, we should start with Ms. Bordeaux and see what she knows—look in the file right there and get the contact number. Ok, try this number: 779-997-4444."

"Hello, you have reached the voicemail of Marla. I can't get to my phone right now. Please leave your name and number, along with a brief message, and I will be sure to get back to you at my earliest convenience. Have a blessed day!"

"Hello Marla, this is Troy Brooks from Brooks and May's Law offices. I have some things I would like to ask you, as well as talk to you about your cousin's case. If you could please give us a call or come down to the office, we would appreciate it," Troy leaves a message.

As Troy is ending the call, his receptionist is buzzing him on the intercom. "Mr. Brooks, I have a Marla Bordeaux on line one."

"Ok, thanks."

"Hello Ms. Bordeaux; this is Troy Brooks. I was wondering if I could have a moment of your time today to stop by and talk to you about your cousin's case."

"Well, I do have an hour or two later this afternoon, around four or four-thirty, to stop by and talk if that works for you," Marla replies.

"Yes, it does work. Well, I will see you then." "Hey Henderson, you have a visitor; let's go." "Who, me? Who is it?"

"I don't know who," the corrections officer replies. "It's a young lady; that's all I know."

The two of them walk down the stairs from Patricia's tier and down a short hallway, where she is placed in front of a TV screen and a phone with a sign by the screen that reads: "The monitor will turn on once the receiver is picked up." Patricia picks up the receiver and it's her seventeen- year-old daughter, Shay.

"What are you doing here? Why aren't you in school? You shouldn't be here!" She yells at Shay.

"Momma, I had to see you; I had to come check on you. Reporters have been following me around all day, taking pictures and trying to ask me questions. Everywhere I go, one of them is there and they shove a camera in my face—

even at school, the kids are all talking and wanting to know what happened."

"Shay, baby—listen to me very carefully. Don't you say another word to anybody! Do you hear me? Nobody!

That animal got what he deserved. If anyone asks you anything, you just tell them to call my lawyer—his name is Troy Brooks—that's all you have to say."

"Momma, what are we going to do? I can't stand to see you here. There must be something that we can do to get you out of here."

"We are working on it, baby girl. I have a bond reduction coming up soon and hopefully my bond won't be too high, so I can post it and be home with you soon. Until then, you must stay strong for me. Don't let those kids or those nosy ass reporters get to you. Nobody needs to know anything, and if you keep your mouth closed, I'll deal with the rest. Do you understand me? Am I making myself clear?"

Shay's tone begins to change and her lips quiver. "Yes, Momma, I understand."

"Shay, listen—you have to be strong out there so I can be strong here. I got this; don't you worry. Momma's got this, and I have you, too. Just don't say anything to anybody. Did you take care of that other stuff like I told you to?"

"Yes, Momma; everything has been taken care of."

"Ok, good. You did good, Shay. I can rest a little better tonight," Patricia says.

"Alright, Henderson—times up. Say your goodbyes; it's time to go back," interrupts the corrections officer.

"I'm coming. Remember what I said, Shay—you don't talk to anyone; not even family! We will get through this, I promise. Love you, baby."

"I love you, Momma!"

"Hello, my name is Marla Bordeaux, and I'm here to see Mr. Brooks."

"Ok, have a seat and I'll let him know you're here." "Hello, Ms. Bordeaux; I'm Troy Brooks. It's nice to meet you. If you would follow me back to my office, so we can get down to the reasons why I called you."

Once settled in his office, Troy says: "Now, Ms. Bordeaux, I'm not sure if you are aware of this or not; however, I went to court on behalf of your cousin Patricia Henderson, per your request. After court, I tried to talk to her about the case and she would not talk to me or tell me what happened—all she said was that it was self-defense, which doesn't give me a lot to go on to build her a defense. I need something more if I'm going to get her acquitted. Do you know how Patricia and Senator Johnson knew each other, or how they met?"

"Well, our family would often host dinners and fundraisers for various charities, so they could have met at one of those events. Before Patricia got married, she would help put on these events. Then, when her husband passed, she became secluded and kept to herself, at least to my knowledge."

"Well, that's a start. Now, wait a minute Bordeaux. Bordeaux…that name sounds familiar. Where do I know that name? I know I've heard it before."

"Our family has been around this town forever, and we have done hundreds of charitable events for this community," Marla states.

"Wait a minute—did you all used to sponsor a baseball team back in the day?"

"Yes, we have sponsored a handful of teams. My father loved baseball, so he always made sure they had whatever they needed."

"I remember, and now I remember where I heard that name before! I used to play on one of his teams."

"Wow, imagine that! What a small world."

"Well, enough reminiscing. If Patricia met the senator back in the day, then that would explain how they could know each other or would have met. Do you by chance keep any type of logbook or records of who attended your events? Or a record of checks people may have written for their contributions to your different charities?"

"I'm not sure; I will have to check with the organization committee. I'm sure that we do keep a log, though."

"Ok, well as soon as you find out, please let me know. I need to find out as much information about them as I can to successfully defend her. Is there anything at all that you can think of that can help me figure this out?" Troy asks.

"No, not really," Marla replies. "Not off the top of my head, anyway. She didn't like to do big family parties or fundraisers. She was more of a homebody, taking care of her family—especially her daughter. They are very tight, and they do everything together."

"Ok, well maybe I should talk with her daughter and see if she can help me at all. Can you set that up for me, please?"

"Yes, I can do that for you. Is there anything else you need me to do for you, Mr. Brooks?"

"No, that's it for now. Thank you; I appreciate it."

"No problem, Troy, it's the least I can do to help you."

"Here is my private number. If you think of anything else, please feel free to call me day or night, it doesn't matter. I'm usually up late and I get up early."

"Ok, well I won't call you too late; I wouldn't want to interrupt you and your wife or girlfriend."

"Well, you don't have to worry about that—I'm not married and I'm not in a relationship right now."

"Really, I'm surprised! A nice-looking guy like yourself with your own practice."

"Yea, well…I was, and things happened. At any rate, I have quite a bit of work that I need to get to. Let me walk you out, and don't forget to get me that information."

JASMINE'S NEW LIFE

Hello Precious. Hey sis, what's up? I was just calling to let you know that I will be late picking up the baby tonight. I'm working on this new murder case and it's going to be a big one. Just to give you a heads up, it may be more long nights. I will try to let you know ahead of time before it gets too late.

"Ok, just let me know. Do you know how late you will be? I need to run an errand and I didn't want to miss you."

"Well, I will call the house or your cell phone before I leave the office to come pick him up."

Jasmine hangs up and in comes Alvin with a smug look on his face. "Jasmine, I hope I'm not out of line here— I know you thought Matt was going to give you this case and that you were going to be the lead prosecutor, but I just want to let you know that I'm glad that you're going to be the Second Chair in this case. It's going to be some late nights coming up. I hope you will be able to manage that along with your baby. I know how rough that can be. Thank God my wife will be home to help with our little princess; I can't imagine what I would do if I had to do it alone and work this job with the hours we keep. Do you know what I mean?"

"Don't worry about me, Alvin; I will be fine! I have it all under control," Jasmine answered.

"I hope so, because I can't look bad on this one. I don't know about you, but I'm ready to get started on this case—we have a ton of work to do. The first thing we need to do is figure out a motive. Why would she kill the senator and how did they know each other?"

"I agree, Alvin; let's put someone on her phone and social media account, and we can put something together to find out if there is any history. Did anyone question the senator's wife to see if she knows anything?"

"I didn't see anything in the file, Jasmine. I will see if I can schedule to have her come in and talk to us."

"That's a good start. I will start with the wife, and you can start looking into Ms. Henderson's background. Well, with that being said, I'm going to take time off so I can get my son. I will let you know what I find out tomorrow."

"Well, you have a good night; I'll be in my office working."

Jasmine makes her way to the car and starts driving. She taps the phone button on the steering wheel and begins to call her sister through her Bluetooth. "Hey Precious, I'm on my way now to pick up the baby. Are you still home or are you out? I can meet you wherever you're at."

"No, sis; I'm at home now. I will get him together and have him ready for you when you get here."

Jasmine slowly walks through the door. "Girl, you will not believe the day I have had today! Where is the wine? I need a big glass after this day."

"What's going on Jasmine? What happened?"

"First, Matt pulls me off the biggest case that this town has ever seen, and then I'm told that I will have to be second chair for Alvin—of all people! Oh, and get this: as we are walking out of Matt's office, he mumbles, 'I don't need a babysitter.' Sis, I thought I was going to lose it on his ass; I was so mad. Then, to make things worse, right after I got off the phone with you, he walks into my office and proceeds to tell me we will be working late and that he hopes that won't be a problem for me because I have a baby, and how fortunate he is to have his wife at home to take care of their baby. I was through then; I had to just gather my stuff and get out of there before I did something or said something stupid. Can you believe the nerve of him? This is not the sixties where men work and women stay home with the babies being good homemakers—we can work and raise a family just like they can."

"Wow, I can't believe he came to you like that! I know you said he was mad about not getting the promotion, but this is a whole new level of pettiness. He had better be glad you kept Jasmine from the projects in check!" Precious laughs. "Pour me a glass of that wine, too, while I check on the baby. He was asleep, so you can stay and eat."

FEELINGS

Two weeks later, Troy is hard at work in his office and Terrance peaks his head in. "Hey Troy, I just heard that Smoove Blu and Jayce will be performing tonight at the A, and I was wondering if you wanted to go check them out and have a drink? We have been putting in a lot of hours these last couple of weeks and I'm sure you could use a break, not to mention we haven't hung out together in what seems like forever."

"You know what? That sounds like a great idea, and I really could use a break to recharge and get out of the house for a while."

"Cool, do you want me to pick you up?"

"No, I'll get you and tonight it's on me. You have held me down all this time; it's the least I can do. I'll be there around eight to pick you up." Troy exclaims.

"Sounds good to me!"

"Man, what am I going to wear? It's been so long since I have been out," Troy says to himself. "Hey, google: play nineties R&B. I might as well get myself ready for tonight. I can tell I haven't worked out in a while; these jeans are fitting a little snug around the waist. I could wear this button up with this blazer. I can make these jeans work with these shoes. Oh, and I have the perfect watch to go with this as well. Ok, Mr. Brooks; I think this will work!" Troy lays everything out across the bed so he can look at what he just put together as he nods in agreement with the ensemble—and of course no outfit of Troy's would be complete without the right scent from his favorite cologne collection. Now that he had everything needed for a great night out in place, all he had left to do was shower and do a quick touch up with the clippers.

Just as the clock hit eight o'clock, Troy pulled up to Terrance's house to pick him up for a guy's night out. Terrance gets in the car, laughing.

"Man, what's so funny?"

"Nothing man, I was just thinking if it's one thing that I have learned about you, my brother, it's that you are always on time. A person could set their watch by you if they wanted to!"

"Nothing wrong with being punctual."

"It's not, bro—I was just messing with you; lighten up."

"I know. It's just been awhile. I haven't been out since Jasmine, and I broke up."

"I get it and tonight will be epic. No more talk about Jasmine, the breakup, relationships, or anything related. Tonight, it's all about fun, drinking, and meeting some new women, right?"

"Right," exclaims Troy.

"Now let the top down and let's get this party started."

Troy spots the owner of the club. "Hey O, what's up man? It's been a minute."

"Yea, it has been. Sorry to hear about your mom."
"Thanks bro, I appreciate it."

"Hey, why don't you and Terrance come up to the VIP section and hang out with me and some of our friends tonight?"

"Sounds good to me. What do you think, T?" "Hey, I'm good with that!"

"Well, let's get to it then. Follow me this way, gentleman," O says.

As the three men walk into the VIP section, it's like a different club up there with different music, people, and atmosphere—the who's who of the city is there. As Troy and Terrance take their seats, a server walks over to the table with two bottles and chasers, compliments of O.

"Well, we didn't come here to sit and look at each other; let's get out and mingle."

"I agree. Let's go this way first and make our way around and see who all is here."

"Hey what's up Troy?" We still need to get together.

"We will," says Troy.

"What's up Terrance?" Nothing much, just out enjoying the night.

"Hey what's going on Mr. Brooks, Mr. Mays; I haven't seen you guys in a long time? Where have you been, are you ready for a drink? "One of the waitresses ask. No, we're good. We already have some drinks set up. Thank you though. Troy politely tells the waitress.

Everyone is speaking and shaking hands with Troy and Terrance, and at this point they both are feeling themselves a little bit with everyone knowing the two of them from their last big case.

Suddenly, Troy catches a glimpse of this beautiful woman from her side view—not really catching her whole face, just the side of her face and the tight form fitting dress she has on. He decided that tonight he would just throw caution to the wind and go speak to her to find out who she is. He eases his way up to the woman and gently taps her on her shoulder.

"Excuse me, would you like to dance?" The alluring woman turns around, and Troy is surprised by who it is—it was Marla Bordeaux. He couldn't believe it; neither could she.

"Sure, I would love to dance with you. I love this song. Smoove Blu is one of my favorite artists."

"Yea, I know; he is the truth." Troy takes Marla by the hand and leads her out to the dance floor. Marla begins to sing the lyrics: "I may not have a million dollars; I may not drive nothing fancy; you're all I need to be happy; you're my version of perfect." At this point, Troy is loving what he is seeing; however, in the back of his mind he understands that she just hired him and how wrong it would be if he said what he was already thinking. Mixing business and pleasure is never a good thing—it's like business 101. However, Marla was looking so good, and this was supposed to be a night of fun and hanging out with no business. Troy is now stuck in a dilemma: Should he keep it professional or throw caution to the wind and go with the flow? Troy being Troy thanks Marla for the dance and politely excuses himself. He finds Terrance back at the table, making himself a drink.

"Man, bro, you will not believe who I was just dancing with. I'll give you one guess." Before Terrance could answer,

Troy tells him. "That was Marla, bro; the one that paid us to take her cousin's case."

"Oh wow, are you serious? That's crazy, bro! So why are you back over here with me? Why aren't you over there talking with her? She is fine!"

"Yea, I know; and she can move on the dance floor—not to mention that perfume that she is wearing is crazy. She smells so good."

"Again, why are you over here with me then?"

"I know, T—that's the business though, and you know how I am about mixing business with pleasure."

"I know Troy, and I get it. We came here tonight to have fun, remember? I saw how she was looking at you in the office and it wasn't about business—that look was about pleasure! Besides, she is not our client—her cousin is. If nothing else, just for tonight go back over there and talk to that woman."

"Yes, you're right. Fix me two of those and I'll be back…maybe," Troy says with a laugh.

"Hey Marla, I hope you don't mind; I got you a drink.

Do you mind if I have a seat?"

"Well, my girl was sitting there, and she just went to the bathroom, so it's cool."

"Well, when she comes back, I'll give her back her seat. What brings you out tonight, Ms. Bordeaux?"

"My girl really likes this place; plus I have never heard Smoove Blu or Jayce in person, so I figured this way I would kill two birds with one stone. What about you, Mr. Brooks? What brings you here?"

"The truth is that it's been awhile since I have been out, and my partner Terrance thought I could use a night out to have some fun. Plus, like you, I have never heard them live either and my friend owns this place."

"Oh, ok are you having fun, then?"

"I am, now—sitting here talking with you." "Oh, really?"

"What does that mean?"

"Oh, nothing; I'm trying to decide if that was genuine or just some line you use," Marla states.

"Trust me, it was genuine. I don't have any lines and I'm too old for games—I'm a straight shooter."

"Ok, I like that—I mean, I can respect that." "Um, excuse me Marla, who do we have here?"

"Lisa, this is Mr. Troy Brooks. Troy, this is my best friend, Lisa."

"Hi, nice to meet you, Lisa. Can I buy you a drink?" Troy asks.

"Sure, whatever you all are having is fine with me." "Ok, cool; I'll be right back. My business partner has a table right over there with a really nice view of the stage, if you both would like to come sit with us."

"Sure, that sounds like fun, Troy."

"Hey Terrance, you remember Marla, and this is her friend Lisa. I hope you don't mind that I invited them to come sit with us to watch the show."

"Of course not; ladies, please have a seat. Can I refresh your drinks?" Just as Terrance was pouring the drinks, a voice comes over the speakers. "Mic check, mic check. One, two, one, two." "How are you all doing tonight? Is everyone enjoying themselves? Ladies, if you're having a fun time, let me hear you make some noise!"

Lisa and Marla both scream, while Marla flashes a smile and eyes Troy. He smiles back at her and looks her in her eyes and asks her for another dance. Troy extends his hand for Marla to take hold as he guides her to the dance floor. Her hand is soft yet strong; she has the grace of an angel as she glides across the room. Troy could see the men as they all looked and stared as they walked by, which made him feel surprisingly good. Troy gently pulls her close as they begin to slow dance. The scent from her perfume is driving him wild. He could tell she works out from the feel of her muscle tone as he gently squeezes her a little tighter to make her feel secure in his arms. Her high heels have her at just the right height for him to be right at her neck, taking in every note of her perfume as they sway back and forth to the beat of the music.

Marla loves how tight Troy has her. She could tell that he works out, as well, from the firmness of his biceps under her hands. She places her arms on the inside of his blazer, running her hands up his back. Everything was right and tight. His cologne was like a magnet for her—she loved the scent of a good smelling man. Troy was everything any woman would want in a man, she thought to herself. He is smart, funny, successful, educated, has a nice body, and has his own money.

As the song heats up, so does Troy and Marla. It had been awhile since Troy was this close to a woman. Their eyes lock and Troy moves in for a kiss; her lips are full; soft, yet firm. He had almost forgotten what it was like to live in the moment and let go while letting your body be free. What starts as a light peck is now a full blown five-alarm enthusiastic kiss; the kind where your heart begins to beat a little faster. The room gets a little warmer, and every nerve in your body begins tingling with excitement. It had been a long time for either one of them to feel a kiss with this much passion; it was the spark that ignited a dormant flame in both of them. Troy, trying to gather his composure, now takes Marla by the hand and escorts her back to the table where Lisa and Terrance are still sitting. Terrance offers them another drink and whispers to Troy. "I thought you could use this after what I just saw," he laughs. Troy grins and catches a look from Marla that suggests that she might be interested in something more. Marla then suggests that they go back to her place to listen to some more music and have a nightcap.

They all agree and walk out together. When Troy and Terrance pull up to the Bordeaux estate, they both are amazed—it's a huge gate with a monogrammed "B" in the middle of it. A buzzer sounds and the gates slide apart to let them in to a long, winding driveway that circles at the end with a multi-colored waterfall display in the middle. In front of the house sat what they assumed was her Maserati with custom made royal blue and white leather interior. Her license plates read "IMBLSSD2." Terrance, being the car guy, was amazed at how beautiful this car was. Troy, although really feeling it, tried to downplay it and play it cool. He rings the doorbell, and an elderly woman answers the door with a maid's uniform on.

"Hello ma'am, we are here to see Ms. Bordeaux." Just as she turns to announce the two of them, Marla comes around the corner and invites them in.

"I thought it would be nice if we sat around in the back by the pool; the pool house is right there, and there are new swim trunks that you can change into in the pool house. Lisa has already changed and I'm going to come down in a few minutes. Please make yourselves comfortable and I'll be right back." Troy eyes her as she slowly turns and walks away. Her dress hugs her in all the right places, and he is excited to see what she looks like in a bathing suit.

Troy and Terrance begin to change clothes in the pool house; there are swim trunks in about every size, along with big, fluffy monogrammed towels with the letter "B" on them. Terrance taps Troy. "Man, can you believe this house? And she has a maid! Man, you hit the jackpot with this one. This house is beautiful."

"I will give you that, T. Not to mention Marla is beautiful and so is Lisa—this could be the best night of our lives tonight."

As they step out of the pool house, Lisa comes over and grabs T and walks him closer to the pool where the lounge chairs are. Troy grabs a seat at the table. Lisa begins to pour Margaritas for everyone and turns on some nice smooth jazz. Out of nowhere, Marla appears in the tiniest bikini imaginable with a see-through covering. They lock eyes and she asks him, "Do you like what you see?" as she does a little spin, giving him a little glimpse of what she is working with. A big lump swells in his throat.

"Absolutely!" Troy grabs her by the hand and gives her twirl so he could get another look at this beautiful woman standing before him. After the twirl, Troy wraps her up in his arms like a Christmas present and leans in for another kiss. Their two bodies look as if they are merging as one— neither one of them can keep their hands off the other. Troy grips her round, firm butt as if he were checking for its ripeness. Marla caresses the back of his head and his chiseled chest, feeling all his muscles. Troy tries to pull away. In his mind he is thinking, "No stop…don't do it!" However, it's too late—it feels too good to stop. He's all in at this point and there is no turning back for either of them.

The night is everything the two of them needed it to be—the music is smooth, the drinks are smoother, and the feel of her body next to his is overriding everything. Lisa and Terrance have now quietly disappeared and it's just the two of them alone. Marla pours the two of them another drink and takes Troy through the sliding glass doors that lead into her bedroom, then slowly removes her cover from her bathing suit, showing off her amazing body with the moonlight hitting all the right angles. This gives Troy all the motivation needed to make this night last forever. He scoops her up and ever so slowly and gently lays her on the bed. The two begin a slow, enthusiastic kiss. She caresses his face while he squeezes her butt; she rubs his arms as he rubs her thigh and begins to untie her thong bikini and top. While he kisses the nape of her neck, she pulls down Troy's swimming trunks. The two begin to make mind-blowing, breath-taking love, as if it were their first time as well as their last into the early morning light.

THE MORNING AFTER

"Good morning, Mr. Brooks; would you like me to get you breakfast?"

"No, that's ok Marla. I must get going so I can get my run in. Thank you for last night! I had a wonderful evening and last night was amazing."

"Yes, indeed. You were amazing, Mr. Brooks. I felt so safe and comfortable with you."

"I know; I felt the same way. The chemistry and vibes were great; it's been awhile since I felt like this, so thank you for an incredible night."

"No, thank you, Mr. Brooks. I'd like to see you again if possible."

"I think we can arrange that. What happened to Terrance and Lisa? I feel like we just forgot about them."

"Oh, they're fine. My driver took them both home last night; I didn't think any of us should be driving."

"Yes, you're right. Those drinks at the club were good and strong, then those margaritas had a nice little kick, too. I must get going now. Can I have a hug before I leave?"

"You sure can; you can have whatever you want, Mr. Brooks," Marla says, as she slides across the bed with nothing on. "Are you sure I can't tempt you to stay? Instead of a run, we can think of another exercise to do."

"As tempting as that sounds and looks, I must get going. Running helps me think and gets me going mentally; I have a lot of cases to prep for."

"Ok, I understand. I'll call you later."

Troy heads home to shower, change clothes, and then to the park. It's been awhile since he's been on a run in the park and it was the perfect day for it; everything seems right in the world again. Troy gets out of his car and begins to stretch and warm up, thinking he would only do about two miles since it has been so long. Minutes into his run, he runs past a woman pushing a stroller with a small child. Troy, not really paying attention, hears this woman calling his name. He couldn't tell who it was because of her baseball cap and mask.

"Jasmine…is that you? I didn't recognize you with the hat, mask, and stroller."

"Yes, it's me, and I know—I hate these masks; however, we still must be careful these days."

"You are right about that. Who is this little guy you have with you?"

"This is my son. Troy, I'd like you to meet Tre." "Wow…are you serious? He's a handsome little guy.

Hi Tre, it's nice to meet you." Troy stares at him for a second—there was something about Tre that looked so familiar to him. The little boy reaches for Troy with his arms outstretched, as if to say, "pick me up," and Troy quickly puts his index finger into the hand of the little guy. Jasmine sees it and moves around the side of the stroller to pick Tre up.

"So how have you been, Troy?" Jasmine asks.

"Um, I'm doing ok; getting back into the swing of things at the office. So, I hear you got the Henderson case."

"Yea, we just entered our appearance in on that case."

"Will you be prosecuting that case?" Troy asks.

"No, I'll be the second chair on it. Alvin will be the lead prosecutor."

"Oh, ok but aren't you—"

Jasmine interrupts, "Yea, I know—it's a long story. Well, it's been a long morning already for him; it's time for his nap. It was good to see you again."

"Yea, likewise! You all enjoy the rest of your day." "Thanks, you do the same."

Troy takes off and starts his jog again then stops again suddenly; he can't shake the feeling of how Jasmine's son looks so familiar—and that little black birthmark on the baby's wrist looks familiar as well. Just then, his phone rings.

"Hello, you have reached Troy Brooks, how can I help you?"

"Well hello, sir. I was just wondering if you wanted to come back to the house for round two. I'll have brunch ready for you," Marla says.

"Unfortunately, I can't—I still have some work to catch up on as well as some errands to run. I'll call you back later and maybe we can get together."

"That is fine, Troy." Click! Did she just hang up on me? What was that all about? Troy thinks to himself. His phone rings again, and this time It's Terrance.

"Hello?"

"Hey, what's up Troy? How did it go last night?" "It was good, we had an amazing time. The question is what happened to you? One minute we were having a drink, and the next thing I know you disappeared."

"Well, Lisa showed me another part of the house and one thing led to another, the next thing I knew it was morning and her driver was dropping me off at home."

"Her driver?"

"Yes, her driver. Not only does she have a house cleaner, but she also has a driver that dropped me off in her Bentley."

"A Bentley?"

"Yes, a Bentley—I knew she had money, but not like this. Man, you hit it big this time. Did you see the rest of that house? It's incredible—from the game room, the bowling alley, the theater room, to the cars and all the staff; everything you could want, she has it. I see."

"Well, that's all fine and good Terrance; however, I'm not impressed with all those things. The only thing I'm concerned about is who she is, and does she have a good heart—the rest is a bonus."

"Yea…yea…yea; I get it, but man, come on—she is rich, filthy rich—and she's fine."

"True that, she is fine—no doubt about that. Anyway, we still have so much work ahead of us with this murder case. We have yet to find out how they knew each other and why she would kill him—that is where our minds should be."

"Ok, Mr. Brooks; you're right. Well, at least I got you out for one night of fun."

"We can celebrate after we win this case. I'm going to finish my run and then do some more research. Glad you made it home safe, T. I'll talk to you later."

As Jasmine begins to place Tre in his car seat, she reflects on seeing Troy for the first time since she moved out, and everything starts to play out in her head. Troy was still looking and smelling good with a body to match; she thought about what would have happened if she had been a better communicator, or if she didn't leave so abruptly, or had not even gone out that night and gotten pregnant—how different her life could be and how she and Troy would still be together. What if Tre was Troy's baby? Just seeing him brought back so many memories of the good times they had together. Even though she doesn't regret having Tre, she still wishes things would have turned out differently. "Oh well, I can't dwell on the past and can't change it either, for that matter," Jasmine says out loud. "Guess we will have to keep it moving, right Tre?" Jasmine sighs ponders all the what if's…and then starts the car.

As much as she would like to stop thinking about Troy, everything on the way home seems to be a reminder of him and the time they spent together. Jasmine is so enamored with the very thought of Troy that she gets out the car and forgets that Tre is in the back seat for a moment, still asleep from the car ride home from the park.

"Oh, baby; Momma is sorry. Let's get you into the house." She lays Tre in the bed and sneaks out quietly, then begins scrolling through her social media accounts. One of her memories pops up, and it's her and Troy in a picture they took together when they first met. All the memories and emotions come flooding back—everything that she thought she had buried or didn't feel any more for Troy is now back—the way he smelled, the way he held her close, his very essence is present in the room with her. The more she scrolls through old pictures on her phone, the stronger the emotions come flooding back, like the tide washing over the beach. One photo stops her and grabs her attention—it's a picture of Troy and his mom when she was in the hospital. Troy is holding his mom's hand, and she notices a black mark on Troy's mom's left wrist. She pinches the screen and makes the picture bigger. The closer she looks at it, the more it resembles the birthmark Tre has on his left wrist—same location, same shape—everything. She runs into Tre's room and gently lifts his arm, examining his wrist. Sure enough, there is that same black birthmark on her wrist that's on his wrist. Her hands begin to shake, and her lips begin to quiver; tears begin to flow as she looks at her baby, as if it were for the first time. Could it be that Tre is Troy's son? There was always something about his eyes that had captured her heart, just as Troy's eyes did when they first met. She quietly slips back out of the room into the hallway, and now she wonders if she made a terrible mistake by breaking up with Troy and leaving the way that she did. Things haven't always been easy, and at the very least Tre, would have a father that loved him and spends time with him instead of this nonexistent father that he has now, who doesn't spend any time with him or help with any of the financial responsibilities because she has neglected to tell him about Tre.

What was I even thinking? Now what do I do? Do I need to do or say anything? Jasmine thinks to herself. I don't think Troy noticed, or he would have said something at the park, or at least called or sent a text by now, I'm sure.

ANSWERS REVEALED

"Good morning, Mr. Brooks. Here is your mail and the briefs that I need you to look over before I send them out."

"Thank you. Is Mr. Mays in yet?"

"No, not yet; he called and said he was on his way.

He had a stop to make before he came in this morning."

"Ok. Can you have him stop by my office when he gets in?

"I sure will. Is there anything else you need this morning?"

"No, that's it, thanks."

Two hours have now passed, and Terrance makes his way into the office. "Good morning, Mr. Mays; Mr. Brooks would like to see you. He is in his office, and I'll put your mail in your office."

"Ok, that would be great. Thank you!"

"Hey what's up, Troy? You wanted to see me?" "Yea, I do; have you heard anything about the Henderson case yet? We have the bail hearing today and I was hoping to have something to work on."

"Unfortunately, I haven't heard anything from the private investigator yet; I was hoping that he might have talked with you. I can reach out to him today and see what's going on."

"Ok, cool. Hey, do you have a second? I want to ask you something," Troy says.

"Sure, what's up?"

"Well, after I got off the phone with you on Saturday when I was doing my morning jog, I ran into Jasmine at the park with her son."

"Oh, how did that go?"

"It was cool. It surprised me, though, to see her with her son. He's a cute little dude and he looks like somebody I know, but for the life of me I can't figure out who. The crazy thing about it, though seeing her again brought back so many memories. I hate that I messed that up; I really think she could have been the one. She was perfect for me!"

"Well, then why don't you reach out to her and see what's up?"

"I can't do that; besides, she has a kid now and so much time has passed. I think she is still with that dude that she cheated on me with."

"Yea, I forgot about that part."

"Yea; I mean, I can understand why she did what she did—I wasn't the best boyfriend at the time, and she was trying to get me to be more open and I just couldn't do it. Now I guess I will just have to live with the consequences."

"Well, at least you got Marla now—that's one way to forget about the past. She's beautiful, smart, fun to be with, and filthy rich—it doesn't get any better than that."

"I don't know, T. She is cool and all, but there is something off about her. I'm getting this weird vibe from her.

I think she may be a little clingy, and I don't like that at all. When I left her house on Saturday morning, I told her that I was going for a run and that I had some work that I needed to catch up on. I wasn't gone an hour before she called and tried to convince me to come back over."

"Man, Troy; maybe she was just lonely sitting in that big house all by herself."

"Yea, I guess. We will see if that's the case, but I'm telling you something is off."

"Yea, ok; you just got Jasmine on the brain now."

"Man, whatever—and did I tell you her son has the same little birthmark, just like Momma used to have?"

"Really? That's odd are you sure that's not your baby?"

"You are tripping. She would have told me if it was mine, right? Anyways, let's get to this bail hearing and see if we can work some magic for Ms. Henderson."

"All rise, please—court is now in session. The honorable Judge Anthony Walker presiding."

"Good morning; you may be seated. Madam clerk, if you would call our first case."

"Calling case number 22CF4237, the people in the state of Illinois versus Patricia Henderson."

"Council, if you would introduce yourself for the record."

"Good morning, your honor; state attorney Alvin Williams for the people."

"Good morning, your honor; Troy Brooks for Ms. Patricia Henderson, who is standing to my left."

"This case is set for a bond hearing, is that correct?" "Yes, sir, that is correct."

"Mr. Williams, I'll hear from you on your recommendation of bail," the judge states.

"Your honor, the state would recommend that her bond remain the same as set. No bond! Ms. Henderson murdered a sitting United States senator in cold blood; she stabbed him multiple times in the chest area and once in the neck, after which she was caught fleeing the scene at a high rate of speed, running a red light, and almost causing an accident. When Ms. Henderson was pulled over, there were some blood stains on her clothing and the murder weapon was found in the trunk of her car, wrapped in a bunch of towels. This was clearly a crime of passion and Ms. Henderson should be locked up with no bond until the time of trial, at which time we will prove her guilty and be asking she receives the maximum punishment allowed: life in prison without any possibility of being paroled. Thank you."

"Your honor, my client denies these allegations," Troy starts. "Your honor, my client is a good person; she has never been in trouble of any kind—not even so much as a traffic violation until that night. She has been an upstanding member of this community all her life; she often volunteers her time to various organizations throughout the city and often donates to various charities; she also runs her own not-for-profit organization for battered women. Her family is very well known here in the city, and her father and uncle have donated millions to the inner-city youth and the city's baseball league—they have been doing this for years. If it weren't for them, I don't know where I would be if it wasn't for their contributions to little league baseball. Yes, Ms. Henderson did have blood on her clothes and the murder weapon in her car; however, your honor, we intend to prove that there is much more to this case than what any of us know. If you look at the pre-sentencing report, you will see that it states she is a minimal flight risk, has significant ties to the community, and a teenage daughter that needs her mother to come home; her daughter is a straight A student who is in her senior year of high school. Your honor, we are prepared to put up one million dollars to secure her release from jail. I know asking for a personal recognizance bond would be a stretch; however, she would be willing to accept any condition of bail that you would consider fit, as well as a curfew and any type of monitoring that you would want. Thank you."

"Mr. Williams, you have the last word," the judge states.

"Your honor, you have the police report—we found blood on her clothes and the murder weapon in her car wrapped up—and she was speeding away from the scene; not to mention that Mr. Craig Johnson has been a Unites States senator for over ten years. It is our belief that her bond should remain the same. Thank you!" "Well, I have considered your arguments and the evidence before me; I've read all the pre-sentencing reports, and I cannot in good consciousness release Ms. Henderson on a personal recognizance bond. Bond will be set at two million dollars. When would you like to come back for a status?"

"Your honor Mr. Mays and I were thinking that we could come back sometime around the end of July to ensure that we would have all the discoveries done."

"Ok, how does July 21st at nine-thirty sound?" "Sounds good, your honor."

"All right, I'll see everyone then. Ms. Henderson, if you do bond out, make sure you go straight to probation and check in with them. That's all. Call the next case."

"Could you please put my client in a conference room for me so we can talk? Thank you."

Troy and Terrance exit the courtroom and head to the conference room.

"Ms. Henderson, we are already getting the funds together to get you out of here; you should be released in a couple of hours. When you're released, you should have enough time to go to probation and check in, and then after that I need to get some more information from you about that night, as well as how you knew Senator Johnson. We must start working on your defense. You heard Mr. Williams—he is looking to keep you locked up for the rest of your life. He would love nothing more than to put you away and put another notch in his belt; he wants to make a name for himself. I'm not going to lie—with the type of evidence that they have on you, it's going to be hard to win unless you tell me something."

"Look, Mr. Brooks, I've told you all that I'm going to tell you—just get me out of here and back to my baby girl; that's all I care about right now. Can you do that, please?"

"Yes, Ms. Henderson; as I told you, we are taking care of that as we speak. Your cousin Marla is paying the bond. Guard, you can take her back now so she can be released. After you get settled at home, we need you to please call our office and set up an appointment; we have a lot to go over."

"Terrance, we have our work cut out for us with this case; I don't think we have ever had a case where our client refuses to help us help them."

"Yea, I know, Troy; this is just mind blowing. Oh, by the way, the private investigator sent me a text and thinks he has a lead; he is going to text me back later with what he finds out."

"Ok cool, finally some good news."

State attorney Alvin Williams is now back at his office throwing a temper tantrum.

"I can't believe that the judge gave her a bond! What was he thinking?! This woman murdered a sitting United States senator…that's almost like an act of treason! This is really an open and shut case; what more do we need to keep this woman in jail? If that were anybody else, I guarantee she would not have gotten a bond. Yet again, people with money get whatever they want—if you have money and rub elbows with the right people, you can get away with murder. Well, not this time! Not on my watch! I'm going to do everything in my power to get this conviction; I don't care who her defense lawyer is."

Jasmine is standing in the doorway, listening to Alvin as he becomes unglued. "Are you finished with your little temper tantrum and talking to yourself now?"

Alvin, slightly embarrassed, straightens his tie and clears his throat. "Why are you just standing there? Do you have information for me, or are you here to gloat that your boyfriend just got his client out on bail?"

"First, you need to check your attitude—I'm still your senior—let's get that straight right now! Secondly, he is not my boyfriend, and don't you ever mention that again. We dated and it's over; I've moved on and I'm sure he has, as well.

"As for news, no—I do not have any news for you. I thought we could go over these phone records that we just received fifteen minutes ago. So, whenever you're done acting like a baby that got his pacifier taken away, you can meet me in the conference room so we can go over these phone records during the time of the murder for Ms. Henderson."

"Now that you have had a chance to cool down, can we get to work now? In looking at her phone records, we see that Ms. Henderson made approximately twelve phone calls around the time of the murder—three of them to her daughter; three to this out of state number; and three to these random numbers. The random numbers all trace back to burner phones. Now, why would someone of her stature be calling someone who uses a burner phone? Maybe she called whoever this person is to help her out of this jam?"

"Hm, that could be it."

"Well Alvin, I have a meeting with the domestic violence team at noon; if you hear anything from the detective or tech team, give me a call."

"Are you leaving already? We still have work to do!"

"Yes, I'm leaving because I have a meeting; I do have other things to do—this is not my only case."

"Yea, yea, yea—don't worry; I can do this case on my own, then."

"Whatever, Alvin—like I said, call me if you hear anything."

"Hey, Marla; did everything go ok with paying the bond?"

"Yes, no problems at all. You know I watched you in court today, Mr. Brooks, and I must say that you were impressive in that courtroom."

"Well, thank you!"

"So, Mr. Brooks, can I take you to lunch?"

"I am busy today. Can I get a raincheck? My schedule is so full; I don't know if I will even get lunch today."

"Come on, Troy—you must eat! And besides, we can talk about my cousin's defense—unless you're just blowing me off; we haven't talked since Saturday night. I'm starting to feel ignored! Did you not enjoy our time together or something?"

"No, it's nothing like that at all—I did enjoy myself. It's just that I have been busy trying to catch up on all the cases that Terrance had to manage while I was dealing with the death of my mother and your cousin's case. Ok, well there is a cafe right around the corner, and we can grab something quick."

"That sounds good to me, Mr. Brooks."

"Good afternoon, my name is Stephanie and I'll be taking care of you today. Can I start you off with something to drink? Or are you ready to order?"

"Marla, do you know what you want?"

"Yes, I'll have a summer salad with a balsamic dressing."

"For you, sir?"

"I'll have the grilled chicken salad with ranch and French dressing."

"Would either of you like something other than water to drink?"

"No, water is fine with me," states Marla. "With me, as well," Troy agrees. "Thank you!"

"This is a lovely place, Troy. Do you come here often?"

"Yea, I guess you can say that. It's convenient for me, with it being so close to the courthouse."

"Oh ok, well I'm glad you decided to come with me. I really thought you were trying to ghost me or something."

"No, of course not; I'm not that type of guy. I really had an enjoyable time Saturday night."

"As did I. I was hoping we could have dinner tonight, if you're available."

Just as Troy was about to answer, he looks up and sees Jasmine walking straight towards him looking like a million dollars.

"Well hello, counselor," Troy says. "Hello, Mr. Brooks, how are you?"

"I'm good. This is my friend Marla, Marla Bordeaux."

"Oh, I know her. We went to college together. I'll leave you to your lunch, Mr. Brooks. You all have a lovely day."

"Oh ok, well you do the same. It was good to see you."

"Wow, that was weird. Was it me or did she seem a little short with me just then?" Troy asks Marla.

"No, it wasn't you—it was her. She has always been that way."

"Really? I've never seen her act that way before with anybody."

"Well, I have. We used to be good friends in college. We spent a lot of time together and did everything together; she was one of my closest friends—until she thought I was after her man. Then she turned on me, and we haven't spoken to one another since."

"Oh wow…ok. That explains why it got so cold in here suddenly. Just so you know, Jasmine and I were in a relationship not that long ago."

"Well, her loss is my gain, I guess. Enough about her; that's old news. Let's talk more about you and me."

"Well, as for tonight, I believe I'm free."

"Great, how about I make dinner tonight around seven?"

"Sounds good to me. You mean to tell me you cook?" Troy chuckles.

"Yes, I cook—just because I have people working in the house doesn't mean I don't know my way around the kitchen."

"Ok, ok—I was just kidding. I hate to cut this short; however, I'm due back in court for some other cases at one-thirty. I'll see you tonight."

"Ok, no hug?"

"Sure, come here." Troy hugs her and Marla gives him a little peck on the cheek and whispers in his ear "until tonight!"

"Shay, Shay…where are you? Mommy's home! Where are you?" Shay comes running from the back of the house, greeting and hugging her mom.

"When did you get out and why didn't you tell me?" Shay asks.

"I would have, baby, but I didn't want you to come down there with all those reporters and news cameras around— they would have been all over you and I didn't want you to go through that. Did you do everything I told you to do?"

"Yes, Momma; I burned the clothes that I was wearing, and I scrubbed my car just like you told me to do."

"Good baby!"

"Now, what are we going to do? Are you going to go to prison?"

"No, Shay, I'm not going to prison; all you need to do is just stay quiet and everything will be ok—just let me manage it all. We have a plan that will take care of everything. How's school going, baby? Have you been staying on top of your grades?"

"Yes, ma'am, and I received a few scholarships offers."

"You did? That's impressive, baby! I'm so proud of you. Pretty soon every university and college will want to have you at their school. I can see it now—the dean calling your name, LaShayla Smith, receiving her juris doctorate degree with a minor in political science. You got all your cords on with a job in hand. Your future is bright baby, and I can't wait to see it."

"Thank you, Momma; I'm going to make you proud!"

"You already have, Shay—never forget that. You're the best thing that I have ever done."

Troy is now on his way back to court for the afternoon call. He has his head buried in his phone and as soon as he looks up the first person, he sees as he walks into the courtroom is Jasmine, hello again, Mr. Brooks—imagine that, running into you twice in the same day."

"I know, right? Hey, Jasmine, I know the way we ended was not ideal and I apologize for that; I never meant to hurt you in any way or push you away—that was the last thing that I wanted to happen."

"It's fine, Troy. We have both moved on and it is what it is; you don't have to explain yourself to me."

"Well, I just didn't want it to be awkward between us."

"It's not!" Jasmine exclaims.

"Well, to me it felt that way earlier when I saw you at the restaurant…or did I misinterpret something?"

"No, it was something, but not what you think. I know Ms. Bordeaux from college, and we used to be friends."

"Oh, really? She told me her version of what happened."

"I bet she did. Look, Troy—you are a great guy and I wish you nothing but the best. I will simply tell you this: be careful, and I'll leave it at that. I need to get back to my office. It was good to see you; take care."

"Oh, come on; you can't leave me hanging like that!

What happened between you two?"

"Troy, I'm sorry. But don't believe nothing she says."

HIDDEN FEELINGS REVEALED

"Hey Clea, come on in and pour you a glass of wine."

"Girl, what's going on? You sounded stressed when you called. I had to come check on my girl."

"You will never guess who I saw today—not once, but twice."

"Who?" Clea asks. "Troy!"

"Your ex, Troy?"

"Yes, he is on the other side of this murder case I'm on. And then get this—I saw him with Marla Bordeaux!"

"Marla, the one we went to college with? That Marla?"

"Yes, the one and only—out of all the people he could have been with. Now, when I walked into the restaurant her back was to me and all I could see was him. So, I walked up to the table to speak to him and there she was, looking all smug and what not. Troy then tries to introduce me to her, and this 'B' rolls her eyes when he is not looking. I almost lost it on her. Then I had to remember that Troy and I are over and have been over, not to mention I'm a state attorney and I was there for a meeting for domestic violence, so it wouldn't look good if I had snatched her up by her weave. You should have seen all the mess she had in her head, and all that makeup with the long, fake eyelashes. I can't believe Troy would even entertain her."

"Could it be that they were meeting because of a case he is working on or she needed some legal assistance? He is a good attorney from what you told me before."

"Yea, that could be. But the way she was skinning and grinning; laughing at everything—I don't think so."

"Now, Jasmine, how do you know all of that and you were in a meeting yourself?"

"Well, I may have glanced over at him once or twice—he looked good in that suit; had a fresh haircut and was smelling good."

"You noticed all that, huh? Jasmine, sounds to me like you got a little jealous when you saw them together—especially since he was with Marla, knowing what she has done in the past with going after your man on the sly when we were in school; that could have triggered something in you that you thought was gone."

"Yea, maybe your right. Oh, he was looking so good! Did I tell you I ran into him at the park a few days ago, too? We talked for a few minutes but nothing serious, and then today he apologized to me for how things ended and that he was sorry for not being more open."

"Wow, how did that make you feel?"

"I mean, it made me feel ok. I wish he could have done that back then; things could be so different—we might have been married by now. If I'm honest with myself, part of me still loves Troy. He's really a good man and has all the characteristics that I would want in a husband. He's good with money; goes to church; is smart, funny, caring, kind— and sexy as hell—if only he could have been more transparent."

"Yea, you still got it bad for him. Why don't you go after him? Let him know how you feel."

"No, I couldn't do that, especially now if he and Marla are an item. He would be a good dad for Tre though. Oh my God…I didn't tell you! The other day when I ran into Troy at the park, I was feeling some type of way, right? I was going through some old pictures—you know how they just show up randomly on your phone—and I saw this picture of Troy's mom when she was in the hospital. On her wrist she has this black spot or birthmark, and Tre has that same mark in the same place on his wrist. I can't remember if Troy has it on his wrist or not, but it is strange, don't you think?"

"Wait a minute, Jasmine—are you telling me that you think Troy could be Tre's dad, like for real, for real?"

"Girl, I don't know; I mean it is possible. Even though we weren't on the best terms, we still got together from time to time, and I just assumed because it wasn't that often that it was my one-night stand. I was drunk and so was he, and one thing led to another; we did what we did and that was it. It never even dawned on me that Tre could be Troy's. Now, with all this time that has passed, I don't even know how I would even explain that to Troy. He was so hurt when I left, on top of losing his mom—now this. He missed the birth of his son; that would really hurt him, and I can't put him through that."

"Jasmine Jones, you're still in love with him, aren't you?" Clea asks.

"You are tripping; I'm not in love with anybody other than my son. I just realize that he's been through a lot and I don't want to add to that."

"Yea, ok. You can only fool yourself for so long, and you for sure can't run from it, especially now."

"Now, what?"

"Well, now you may have a constant reminder every time you look at Tre; you're going to wonder 'am I robbing him from a chance to have a real father in his life? Did I make a mistake by leaving Troy?' If you don't deal with these things, you will be hiding from these things forever.

You know time often has a way of revealing things we don't want others to know."

"That's true! Ever since I saw that picture and looked at Tre's wrist, I have been having all these thoughts and what if moments. I've got to figure this thing out before it drives me crazy. Thank you, sis, for keeping it real with me and giving me some much-needed advice."

"Any time; that's what we do. We hold each other up, straighten each other's crowns, and be there for one another."

"Yea, your right. I need to figure out the right way to go about it; it's not like I can just go to Troy and tell him Tre might be his because he has a birth mark on his wrist—not to mention we are on this trial against each other. Alvin would love for me to get kicked off this case—or if my office found out and we lost this case, everyone would have a field day and I'm sure they would throw me under the bus! They already think that I don't deserve it because of my age and because I'm a black woman. No one saw the late nights and early mornings I spent on my cases, learning every detail of every case that I was assigned; how I've studied case law after case law and all the statutes that apply—not to mention my win-loss record in the courtroom. I deserve to be where I'm at because I've busted my butt and worked hard."

"You don't have to tell me, sis. I already know and you're right. Listen, don't allow anyone to steal your joy or put you down. If there's one thing I know for sure, it's that God has a plan for all of us, and he didn't bring you this far for nothing. He has always guided you in the right direction; just continue to trust him and everything will work out for you. If you need me just call."

"I know, sis, and thank you—I needed to hear that today."

"Anytime. Give Tre a hug and kiss for me." "I will. Take care."

Troy pulls up to the long winding driveway of the Bordeaux estate and the maid greets him at the door.

"Good evening, Mr. Brooks." "Good evening."

"Ms. Bordeaux is in the billiards room right down this hall, the second door on your left." Troy opens the door and walks into the billiard room. Marla is bending over the table, taking her next shot with a short miniskirt and heels on. She turns around and her button up shirt is unbuttoned down to her navel with no bra on.

"Do you play, Mr. Brooks?"

"Yes, I've been known to play a little."

"Well, let's see what you've got, shall we? Would you like a drink?"

"Sure, I'll take a shot of whiskey if you have it, with a few cubes of ice." Jasmine takes one of the ice cubes and slowly runs her tongue over the ice cube in a teasing fashion. Troy smiles and watches with intent. She grabs another one and runs it down her chest exposing some of her breast and then turns away to grab Troy's drink and hands it to him. She notices the bulge that is now protruding in Troy's slim fit pants.

"Ok, here you go." "Thank you!"

"Do you play eight ball, Troy?" "Sure do; last pocket wins."

"Ok sounds good."

"So, Marla—when we were at lunch today and Jasmine Jones came over to the table, why did I sense this weird vibe? I ran into her again after lunch at the courthouse, and she told me to ask you."

"Troy, if you don't mind, can we talk about anything else other than her? The night is young, and we have a wonderful meal planned for us. Let's just play pool, drink, eat and have some fun."

"That all sounds great and all; however, what all happened with you and Jasmine back in college? I know you said you fell out over some guy but what happened?"

"Well, back in college, Jasmine and I were best friends. We met during our first year and we were dorm mates. We grew really close to the point that we did everything together. On summer breaks, she would come here and hang out, or when my family went on trips, she would come with us— there was nothing that we didn't share with one another. Then, our senior year, she started dating this one guy. He was a cool guy that everyone liked; he was quiet and kept to himself—or so we thought. One night, he and Jasmine had gone out bar hopping, and I had gone out to a frat party with some friends. I had come home before them because I had way too much to drink and was going to have my friend come over. Well, while I was waiting for him to come over, I must have passed out on the couch, and that's when Jasmine and her boyfriend came in. Next thing I know, I feel the covers slowly starting to be removed off me and a hand gripping my ass. I assumed Jasmine had let my friend into the apartment and it was him, so we are making out on the couch. Next thing I know, the lights come on and Jasmine is standing over us, yelling, screaming, and hitting him—the whole time I'm still drunk and oblivious as to what is really going on. He finally leaves and she then starts going in on me, telling me how I was wrong and that she knew that I wanted him, and how I dressed provocatively in front of him on purpose and all these crazy things. Two days later, she moved out and we haven't spoken since. I tried to reach out to her several times since those college days, but she must have blocked me. I know that I did nothing wrong that night, so I'm over it—she can think and feel whatever about me. Sorry that I dropped all that on you, but you asked, and I tried to tell you that I didn't want to talk about it."

"Thank you for explaining that to me." Troy, now feeling a temperature change in the room, beckons Marla to come over to him and he hugs her tightly. "I appreciate you telling me that. I do not like secrets, and I understand now how hidden feelings have a way of coming back to haunt us if not dealt with." The two begin to kiss passionately. Troy gently caresses Marla's face and neck with both hands, then suddenly picks her up and places her on the pool table. Just as things begin to get hot and heavy, there's a knock at the door. It's the housekeeper, letting them know that dinner is ready. Troy takes a step back to adjust himself before helping Marla off the pool table.

"Let us continue this a little later, Mr. Brooks."

"Yes, indeed," he replies. She takes Troy by the hand and leads him to the dinner table. Troy, always the gentleman, seats Marla and then takes his seat. The two hold hands while Troy says grace. "Troy, I want you to know that I'm usually not like this with every man that I meet. I'm at an age where now I look to date with a purpose; I value myself and I know my worth—I only go after what I see value in. You are a great guy and a true gentleman. I'm not trying to pressure you to answer or anything like that; I just thought you should know upfront what I'm looking for."

"Oh ok; well I can appreciate you being upfront and honest with me—this is a first for me."

"I'm not looking for any type of answer right now."

"Ok, well I will tell you this: I'm also looking to date with a purpose. I don't sleep around, nor am I into one-night stands. I tend to love hard, and when I'm committed, I'm committed."

Marla is now smiling from ear to ear, as if she just won a hundred-million-dollar jackpot in Troy. She leans in for a kiss. "Oh, I have something for you. Here is a list of everyone who has attended our fundraising events over the years. If the senator and my cousin were ever there together at the same time, they would have had to sign in here; this is how we kept track of who came so that we could send out mailers for future events."

"Well thank you; I appreciate that. Hopefully, we can start putting some pieces of this puzzle together. Anyway, that's enough about work—I don't want your food to get cold. This smells amazing."

MOMMY DAUGHTER TIME

"Good morning, Shay, how did you sleep last night?" Patricia asked.

"Good morning, Momma. To be honest with you, every time I closed my eyes all I could think about is what happened—all that blood, and him on top of me and hurting you."

"It's ok, baby! I'm fine, you're fine, and we will be ok. What do you think about us spending the day together tomorrow? We can wake up, grab some breakfast, and then do some shopping and get a manicure and pedicure, then after that we can catch a movie and dinner, wherever you want to go."

"That sounds wonderful, Momma. It's been awhile since we did that."

"I know Shay, and I apologize for that. We both have been so busy with everything going on in our lives. How's school going?"

"It's going alright; some days are better than others. My grades are good and I've gotten a few colleges acceptance letters. I'm still waiting for one, though."

"Oh, I can guess which that one is! Georgetown, right?"

"Yes ma'am! That's my dream school right there; their criminal justice and law programs are some of the best in the country—it's also one of the hardest to get into."

"Well, if they're that good and hard to get into, they will be lucky to have my baby girl. You have been preparing for this since you were a little girl. You have taken all the right classes, not to mention all that volunteer work you have done—you deserve to be there; just stay focused on what's in front of you and I will take care of the rest. Momma loves you baby, and we will do everything we can to ensure you get in. As for tonight, what would you like to eat and do?"

"I was thinking that we could order some pizza, eat some ice cream, and watch some movies."

"That sounds like a plan. Do you want a meat lovers or barbecue chicken pizza?"

"Either one is fine. I need to finish some homework; by the time it gets here I will be done with everything that I need to do."

"LaShayla, pizza is here."

"Ok, Momma; be right there."

"Do you want something to drink?"

"Yea, I'll have some lemonade, please. Momma, can I ask you something?"

"Yes, baby, you can ask me anything."

"I have the feeling that you knew Mrs. Johnson personally."

"Why would you say that?"

"I noticed that you kept calling her by her first name, Michelle."

"Oh yea. Well, I knew her from back in the day. We met when I was working at the clinic. Why do you ask?"

"I was just wondering."

"Well, stop wondering and asking questions—the less you know is better for all of us. Now can we watch this movie? I heard it was surprisingly good."

The next morning, Patricia asked her daughter: "LaShayla, are you ready?"

"Yes, I'm ready, Momma."

"Ok, good—let's go, I'm starving. I thought we could start with breakfast, then go to the city for some shopping."

"Sounds good to me—you know I love shopping."

"Yea, I know; you are your mother's child!" They both laugh and head out the door.

"Good morning, ma'am, will it be just the two of you?"

"Yes."

"Ok, great! Follow me this way. Would you like a booth or a table?"

"Booth, if possible."

"Ok, great! Here are your menus and your server will be right over."

"Sounds good, thank you."

"I love this place; their food is so good. I want an omelet with pancakes. What about you Shay what are you going to have?"

"I don't know yet; I'm thinking about this skillet breakfast."

"Excuse me, Ms. Henderson; how are you? I'm sorry to bother you while you're having breakfast; however, I still need to meet with you."

"I know Mr. Brooks, and I promise I will call and make an appointment."

"Ok, thanks. I'll let you get back to your breakfast. Oh! Mr. Brooks, this is my daughter, LaShayla—but we call her Shay."

"Hello Shay, it's nice to meet you. You ladies take care and enjoy the rest of your day."

"You do the same."

"Mom, he is fine, and that suit was nice. Who is he?" "Mr. Brooks is my attorney, honey."

"Oh ok. Mom, you need to make that appointment and meet with him."

"I know, honey; I've had to do some other things, as well."

"But Momma, this is important."

"I know that! These other things were just as important, as well. I told you; I got this. You just focus on school."

"Alright, ladies; who had the omelet? There you go, and here's your skillet. Is there is anything else I can get either one of you?"

"No, it looks like we have everything. Thank you."

SECRETS REVEALED

"Hey T, when you get a chance, can you step into my office for a minute?"

"Sure, what's up Troy?"

"Well, last night I was having dinner with Marla, and she gave me a list of all their family events along with their guest lists for the past fifteen years or so."

"Ok, now, what are we looking for exactly?"

"We need to figure out how Ms. Henderson and Senator Johnson knew one another and what could be her motive for killing him."

"While we are going through this, our private investigator says he may have something, as well, and he will get back to me sometime this morning."

"I hope he does—we need something since she is not cooperating. I ran into her and her daughter this morning while I was getting breakfast; I reminded her that she needs to come and talk with us, but I got the feeling she was blowing us off."

"Why do you think she would do that?"

"I'm not sure, T, but something is just not sitting right with me and this case. My gut is telling me she is hiding something, and I've learned over the years to trust my gut."

"I'm with you; it hasn't led us astray in all these years."

"Let's dig into these papers and see what we can produce."

"Troy, these papers read like some type of celebrity A list—every big name in the city has attended these events. I can only imagine the amount of money these have brought in over the years."

"Do you remember that little league baseball team we played on?" Troy asks.

"Yea, I remember."

"The Bordeaux family sponsored that team, as well as the league."

"Oh really?!"

"Yea, Marla was telling me all about it. Oh my God, T, all this time we have been looking for Patricia Henderson—but her family name is Bordeaux!"

"Ok, now we are getting somewhere! Patricia attended all these fundraisers and charity events; she even chaired a few of these. However, I don't see the senator's name at any of the events. What happens when dignitaries can't make an event? They usually send someone in their place right. What if the senator did the same thing? What if he sent someone in his place? T, do me a favor and do a search on Senator Johnson's aid for the last fifteen years or so."

"It says that Michelle Leaper was and currently still is."

"Whoa, wait a minute! In these earlier years, Michelle Leaper did attend most of these events—then suddenly, she stopped coming; I don't see her name anymore. I do see Michelle Johnson's name appearing on the sign in sheets, the same year the senator got married, that could be the connection. Patricia didn't know the senator personally; however, she does know his wife."

"Even if that is true, how does that help us?"

"I'm not sure yet, T. It's more than what we had before, so at least it's a start."

"Yea, that's true. Also, thank you for coming in on a Saturday to help me out with this; I really appreciate it."

"Hold on one sec, Troy; this is Mike, the PI we hired."

"Hey, what's up Mike; what do you have for me?" "I talked to one of the guys who did the valet parking that night, and he told me that at some point during the evening, Ms. Henderson rushed out to get her car and didn't want him to take it to the front entrance. She got the keys herself and drove it to the side of the building; it looked like she picked up another woman and then they sped off. About an hour later she came back, and the valet parked like normal. I did some more digging and checked into some hotels, right? Thinking this might be a random hook up or something they wanted to keep on the DL. So, after going to a few hotels and showing her picture, I found out she did check in at Best Nights Suites. She did not stay though; she got the room and left. Whoever she was with stayed the night and then called a car service in the morning. Now, when the cleaning crew went to clean up that morning, they noticed some blood in the bathroom shower and on the bed. I will keep digging, though—just wanted to let you know what I have so far."

"Thanks Mike, talk to you soon! Wow! Did you catch all that, Troy?"

"Yea, I did, and man—what did we walk into here?"

"We need to get a timeline set up with everything we know right now, and hopefully we will get the rest of the information from Ms. Henderson."

"The first thing is that we know Ms. Patricia Henderson, formerly Boudreaux, has known Mrs. Michelle Johnson—formally Leaper—for some time through various charity events. On the night of the murder, Ms. Henderson left at some point during the night. She got her car from the valet area and drove to the side of the building to pick up another woman, which could have been Mrs. Johnson, and proceeded to the Best Sleep Suites—she checks in but never goes in. Then, Mrs. Johnson—who is bloody—goes into the room where we found blood in the bathroom as well as the bed. She then calls for a car service to pick her up in the morning. An hour later, Ms. Henderson comes back to the party using the valet services like nothing has happened."

"Why would Ms. Henderson do all these things if she did or didn't kill the senator? It doesn't make sense; we are still missing something here."

"Troy, I'm just taking a wild swing here, however, do you think that Ms. Henderson and Mrs. Johnson were having some type of affair, then the senator found out about it and that's why the senator was killed? A crime of passion? He found out about it, the two women leave, then Ms. Henderson comes back. She and the senator get into it again and they fight, then she kills him. We could say that it was self-defense."

"Hm, that's a good theory, T. The only thing though is I don't see Ms. Henderson liking women for one, and two, that doesn't explain the blood in the hotel room."

"What if they both got into the car and that's why Ms. Henderson didn't stay at the hotel? That would explain the blood in the hotel, and Ms. Henderson leaving then going back to the charity event."

"Ok T, we have been going at this for hours now. Let's step back, get clarity, and come back Monday with fresh eyes. Excellent work today! I feel better now having something to work with."

"Agreed, sounds like we have a plan. Let's go grab something to eat and see if we can catch some games on TV."

"Jasmine, it's me, Alvin. We may have caught our first break in the case. I'm here at the office now, and I need you to come in so we can look at this video and discuss our next move."

"Alvin, you do realize it's Sunday, right? Not to mention I have my son with me—we can discuss this tomorrow morning."

"No one will ever be able to say that I didn't put my job first. Enjoy your day; I'll be here working."

"What is that supposed to mean, Alvin?"

"Nothing; you go ahead and do you, and I'll be here working."

The call ends: Jasmine is furious with Alvin and heads to Precious's house to see if she can watch Tre for a few hours. When she pulls up, Precious can see her visibly upset.

"Girl, what is wrong with you? Your hands are shaking," Precious asks.

"It's that smug ass Alvin, my coworker. We just got a lead on this case that we are working on together and because I didn't drop everything, I had going on today, he tried to make it seem like I don't care about my job or this case like he does. Hell, he can only do that because his wife stays at home and doesn't work. He has no idea of what it's like to be a single parent with responsibilities; I can't just drop everything I have going on like he can. Anyway sis, let me get going and go handle this—I'll be back as soon as I'm done. Everything he needs is in his bag. I really appreciate you keeping him for me on such short notice."

"It's no problem, sis. You know I got you."

"I have got to run before Alvin turns this into a big deal and tries to somehow make me look bad." Jasmine angrily slams the door and calls Alvin. She tries her best to calm her nerves before speaking to him to avoid saying the wrong thing and becoming unprofessional.

"Alvin, this is Jasmine. I'm on my way into the office and we need to get a few things straight when I get there."

"Ok, Alvin; I'm here and we need to talk! One thing that we will not do in this office is to be disrespectful. You may be the first chair on this case, but you still report to me, so you will respect me as such. From now on when you talk to me, you will talk to me with respect as your direct supervisor. As for me being a single parent and not being able to drop everything to come running into the office, that's not always going to happen. I'm a single parent and my son comes first. If my boss doesn't have a problem with it, then you shouldn't either—I do my job and I do it very well. Let's not forget that I would have been the first chair on this case; but since I'm not, we will work together and get this case resolved. Now that we have an understanding, let's get to work. Alvin now speechless as if he was just hit with a body shot from a heavyweight fighter that can't catch his breath and just sits there struggling to find his next move. What did you find out?"

"There is a video of Ms. Henderson leaving in the middle of the party with someone else. Now, we can't see the other person's face just yet; the tech is still working on it. We also found out that she drove to a local motel and checked in but never went into the room. The detectives are talking to the clerks as we speak."

"What would make her leave in the middle of the party?"

"Hm…what if she left the party after she killed him? Whoever this other person is that left with her must have helped her."

"Or we could have it all wrong. Ms. Henderson is the one who helped cover up the murder and this mystery person is the one who killed the senator—which would explain why she had blood on her clothing when Ms. Henderson was arrested, and why she checked into the hotel alone. That way, this other person is not on any camera. We need to go over who all attended this event again, from the workers to every dignitary—every single person. We must be missing something or someone."

"Alvin, we have been at this for hours now; I think it's time we stopped for the day. We can start building a viable scenario around the information we have gathered and maybe come up with a motive tomorrow. We got a lot accomplished today, Alvin."

"Wow, is that a compliment?" Alvin asks.

"Look, I always give credit when credit is due and you are a good attorney—no one can take that away from you. It's the way you treat others that is the problem."

"Well, have a good night and I'll see you in the morning."

"Yea, good night; I'll see you tomorrow."

PAINS FROM THE PAST

"Good morning, Mr. Brooks. Here is your morning paper, your mail, and your calendar for the day—it's not too bad for a Monday. Oh, and Ms. Henderson called; she will be here in about an hour for her appointment."

"Cool, thank you. Is Terrance in yet?" "Yes, he's in his office."

"Knock, knock! Hey, are you going to be busy in the next hour or so?" Troy asks Terrance.

"No, I'm not; just going over some briefs and case law. Why, do you need something?"

"Ms. Henderson finally made an appointment to come in and talk, and I want you to be there with me—this case is going to take both of us to win."

"Whatever you need, I got your back."

"I already know. How was your weekend?"

"You know me—it was entertaining. I went to the cigar lounge for a little bit. I found my new favorite cigar; it's smooth and has a nice, slow burn. I'll have to get us some. After that, I went back to Club A and listened to these two local bands. I had never heard them in person before— the one group had this one lady lead singer who could blow. She sang some old and new school jams. Then, the last group were these three brothers—or cousins, or something like that—they could sing and they put on a show. You would have enjoyed yourself. After that, I got a call from Marla's friend from the other night and…well…you know the rest," Terrance smiles.

"Yea, I already know. I'm glad you had a good weekend and had some fun."

"Excuse me, Mr. Brooks; Mr. Mays; Patricia Henderson is here to speak to you. I have her in the main conference room waiting for you."

"Ok thanks; we will be right there."

"You ready T?" "Yea, let's go."

"Hello, Ms. Henderson; this is my partner and co-counsel, Terrance Mays. He will be helping me with your trial."

"Hello, it's nice to meet you, Ms. Henderson," Terrance says.

"It's nice to meet you, too, Mr. Brooks," Patricia says. "I need to ask you one question before I say anything else—because you have been paid and you're officially my attorney, whatever I tell you is confidential, right?"

"Yes, whatever you tell either one of us is confidential."

"I didn't kill the senator and I can't tell you who did. Yes, his blood was on my clothes and my prints on the murder weapon, but that was because I tried to help him. When I pulled the letter opener out of his neck, his blood started squirting everywhere—I couldn't stop it. Although that animal got what he deserved, I didn't want him to die like that, which is why my fingerprints are on the murder weapon and his blood all over me. After that, we got our coats, and I took my friend to a hotel so that she could gather herself."

"Ok, wait—let's go back to the beginning. How did you know the senator?"

"I met him years ago when I was a teenager; he used to come to the fundraisers that my dad would have for some of the local politicians. The senator was then an up-and-coming alderman. My dad really liked him and started mentoring him. Every day, he would come over to see my dad. Some days, he would come over early when no one was home, and we would have these long, deep conversations. One day he came over and…and…and," Patricia hesitated. "He started touching me and kissing me. I told him to stop, but he wouldn't. He kept insisting that he knew that's what I wanted; he kept saying it repeatedly. The more I resisted, the more aggressive he got. He was so strong. The next thing I knew, he was ripping my panties off and forcing himself inside me. I couldn't move or scream or do anything. All I could do was lay there. When he finished, he got up, got dressed, and told me that I better not tell anyone; that no one would believe me because I was just a teenager and he was an up-and-coming politician that everybody liked—including my father, who was mentoring him—and how if I told anyone my dad would look bad. After that, I just remember showering and curling up on my bed. From that day forward, I made it a point to never be in the same room with him; I would always find an excuse to leave the room.

Years later, I was working at the shelter for battered and abused women, and this woman comes in after she was beaten half to death by her boyfriend. She looked like she had been in a war—both eyes had been swollen shut. She had broken ribs, a broken arm, and a concussion. Over time, we became close. Then one day, she just up and vanishes.

"A few months go by, and my dad is having this huge birthday party when in walks my friend, looking like a million dollars. She has on this long, expensive gown, some red bottom heels, and this beautiful diamond necklace. As soon as I saw her, I immediately went over to see her. We hugged and greeted each other like long lost friends, and then she introduced me to her fiancée. My jaw dropped and my heart began to race—I was shaking, I was so mad—and he acted like he didn't even know me. It was then that I put two and two together—he was the one who had beat her, putting her in the shelter. I never said anything to my friend that night and once again excused myself from the room. The next time I saw him was the night he died. I was talking with some friends, and they told me that they had seen my daughter come in, but they hadn't seen her in a while. I went looking for her. I had looked everywhere except for the office so when I opened the office door, I saw that he had my baby pinned down on a desk with her shirt half unbuttoned and her ripped panties were on the floor. I lost it and went after him. I managed to get him off her, but he was so strong.

He then had me pinned down on the ground and was choking me when my friend came out of nowhere; he was in such a rage that night, like he was high on something. She hit him and tugged at him, and he would not budge. I was at the point of almost passing out and then she stabbed him with the letter opener. He finally fell over, and I tried to help him. I removed the knife and tried to put pressure on his wound. She must have hit an artery or something because there was so much blood coming from him; I knew there was nothing else we could do for him. I told my daughter to fix her clothes and to go home while my friend and I left outside the back entrance; I drove her to the hotel so she could get cleaned up."

Troy and Terrance can't believe what they're hearing; neither one of them had any idea that the senator was like this.

"If you do not mind me asking, why was your daughter there in the office with him? How did she know him?"

"I didn't know that she did until I got out of jail. Shay told me that she had been working on his campaign, running errands and doing some computer work for him, creating surveys and what not. That night, she needed him to sign some papers, so she stopped by his office to get his signature.

She said he had been drinking and his speech was very slurred and you could smell the alcohol on his breath. He kept trying to kiss her and she kept saying no! Next thing you know, he had picked her up and pinned her on the desk. I guess that's when I walked in and went after him." Shay was visibly shaking, and tears were flowing down the side of her face.

"I am so sorry you all had to go through this; however, we need to know who your friend is. I know who it is, but I need you to tell us who is your friend. What's her name?" Troy asks.

"First, I need to know if I can trust you—I'm putting my life on the line here and in your hands. I have never told anyone this story, except for my friend when I was taking her to the hotel."

"Yes, Ms. Henderson, you can trust us."

"My friend is the senator's wife. He has been beating her for years and cheating on her. When she was at the shelter, he reached out to her using one of those social media apps and he somehow convinced her that he would change and go to counseling so they could get married. He did that for some time—or at least he pretended to do it—and next thing you know, they're married and he's beating her again. He controlled the money, so she had nowhere to go and nowhere to turn; so she stayed in the marriage. When she saw him on top of me, choking me, she snapped. If you could see the look in her eyes, it was like her spirit had left her body and she was just an empty shell. She never said a word the entire ride to the hotel—she just sat there, looking at the blood on her hands in this catatonic state. Even when it was time to go into the hotel room, I had to help her walk into the room."

"Wait, wait, wait—let me get my head around all of this. Senator Johnson sexually assaulted all of you?"

"Yes, that animal assaulted all of us. I was too ashamed and embarrassed to tell anyone and so was his wife. The only reason I knew about it was because I was at the shelter that night when she came in—if not for that, she would never have told anyone."

"Well, what about your daughter? How did she end up working for the senator?"

"She had a class project where she had to volunteer for a local campaign and then write a report on her experience. She never told me which campaign she was working on; had I known, I would have never let her work for him. I can't believe I let this happen to her. I'm her mother and I'm supposed to protect her from guys like that— I should have been there for her. How did I let this happen?"

"Ms. Henderson, it's not your fault—you didn't know that this was going to happen. You can't blame yourself for his actions."

"No, you're wrong—it is my fault; had I said something all those years ago, this would never have happened to my baby or his wife. He should have been put away years ago, like the animal he is or worse—six feet under. He got what he deserved, and I hope he burns in hell for what he did to us."

Troy takes her by the hand and tries to calm her down. "Ms. Henderson, I need you to calm down and you cannot say things like that aloud, especially in public. Despite how you feel about him, the rest of the city loved the senator. I must be honest with you—this case will be hard for us to win if we can't tell the whole story. I'm not saying we can't win it; I'm just saying that we have our work cut out for us. Why don't you go home and get some rest while we try to think of a strategy to win this case?"

"Wow T, can you believe this? Do you think she is telling us the truth?"

"I mean, I've heard some wild stories in my time, but this is unbelievable."

"True, but bruh—domestic violence is real and running rampant in this country. Did you know that one out of every three women, and one out of every four men, have experienced some type of domestic violence by an intimate partner? One in twenty-five are injured by an intimate partner; mind you, these are just the reported numbers. I'm sure there are more out there that haven't reported or said anything. So, as crazy as it sounds, I can't say she is lying. We should remember that a lot of women have been beaten for years and are hurting on the inside while moving on with life, because they're either to scared or too embarrassed to say anything. The numbers are scary, and to think you can see the person smiling and appearing happy but behind closed doors they are living a life of pain."

"That is so true—we never really know what's going on behind closed doors."

"Man, don't I know it. All those years that have gone by and I never knew how much I was holding on to until I started going to therapy. Once I started talking more, the more I unpacked, from my childhood until now; layers upon layers of emotional baggage that I carried. Now that I've heard their story, my story doesn't even compare. Not that I am comparing, but you know what I'm saying—those two ladies have been carrying all that pain for years, and then to see the same man who hurt you doing it to someone else— and a child at that—I would have snapped, too!" "Wait a minute, that's our angle; that's how we can play this. If we can get a jury made up of mostly women and get them to understand what she was going through, they will understand how all of this played out."

"Our client was abused as a teen. She then befriends someone who was in a comparable situation with the same person, and finally walks in on that man assaulting her daughter—who wouldn't have snapped in that moment and defended their child? Now, if we get some men on board who are fathers with daughters, especially teenage daughters, they will understand, as well, since fathers are natural protectors of their families. They will side with us. I believe we could win this case now."

"Troy, I don't know how you figured out this stuff so quickly. We had nothing a few minutes ago and now we have a strategy and plan on how we can win this. I'm glad I'm on your side and not opposing council. Speaking of, how are you going to deal with Jasmine?"

"What do you mean, how am I going to deal with Jasmine? She works for the state and I'm working for our client. She is opposing council—that's it, that's all."

"Ok, Troy; you can tell that to anyone else other than me—I know you still have feelings for her and when you see her, she makes you feel some type of way. You were a perfect couple. So, seeing her every day for hours on end when the trial starts won't be easy, especially if she comes into the courtroom looking how she be looking. That's got to do something to you."

"Ok, T ok. Yea, if I'm honest with you and myself, she does make me feel some type of way and it is hard to see her and not want to be with her. She's an amazing woman and any man would be lucky to have her. However, I'm not that man, and I have a job to do with a lot at stake for us personally and professionally. I'm sure we will have a lot of people watching us on the news."

"That's true, but Troy—if there was any possibility that you and Jasmine could get back together, would you do it?"

"I honestly don't know. She has a kid now—not that it matters to me—then everything that happened that we never dealt with…there is a lot to unpack there."

"If it were me, I think I will give it another shot."

"I know my mom would have been happy to see us together; she really liked her. No matter what, though, Jasmine will always have a special place in my heart. Now, can we get back to work please?"

"I'm just checking on you to see where your head is; I'm always looking out for my brother."

"I know and I appreciate you for that; I know I can always count on you."

REVEALED

"Hello Troy, this is Jasmine. I need to talk to you about something and I would like to do it face to face if that is ok with you."

"Sure, I guess. What do you want to talk about?"

"Well, I would rather talk in person and then I can tell you."

"Ok, where would you like to meet?"

"That's the hard part, especially with this trial coming up—I don't think meeting at either of our places would be good."

"Well, what if we meet at the park? You remember that spot where we first met? How about there?"

"Ok, that will work. Do you still run? I haven't seen you down there in some time."

"I do; however, it's been awhile. I've been busy at work and then with Tre—I try to spend as much time with him as I can."

"Oh ok, I can understand that."

"What time would you like to meet? How does this Saturday at eight-thirty sound? That will give me time to get him to a babysitter."

"Ok, sounds good." An awkward silence hits them both.

"I'll see you on Saturday, Mr. Brooks."

"Yea, I guess you will. It was nice hearing from you Jasmine; take care and I'll talk to you later. Have a good day."

Jasmine hangs up with Troy and immediately calls her sister, Precious.

"Hello?" Precious answers.

"Hey sis, you won't believe what I just did." "What did you do?"

"Girl, I called Troy and I think I'm going to tell him about Tre."

"Are you serious? You didn't!?"

"Yes, I did, and we are meeting on Saturday at the park. I think it's only fair that he knows that at least it's a possibility Tre might be his son—at least we can get things started by finding out who exactly his dad is before he gets too old."

"Sis, are you sure you want to do this, especially right now? I mean, your job and all the pressure they're putting on you—then you have this trial with him being opposing council. Not to mention your still in love with this man! I think you should wait at least until this trial is over. After that if you still feel the same way, then by all means talk to him. That's just my two cents; either way I know you will do what's right and best for everyone."

"I hear you, sis, but I already made the call and told him that I wanted to meet so that we could talk."

"Well, just make up something and see if you can get him to take a plea or if there is a way to settle this case or something—you know, do what lawyers do. Or you can call and postpone the meeting; tell him something came up."

"Yea, I hear you sis, and you're right. I just don't want my baby to grow up and not know his father. Not to mention if it is Troy's, they have already lost so much time with one another—I would hate for them to waste more time because of me."

"Jasmine, take some time to think about this. It's only Tuesday and you're not supposed to meet until Saturday, so you have time to think about it."

"Yea, you're right. I will take some time and think about this more. Thanks sis, I feel better now. I hate the thought of blowing him off, though—I was low key looking forward to seeing him. The last time I saw him he was looking and smelling good as always. Unfortunately, he was with that Marla…but anyways. If I do decide to meet him, can you watch Tre for me?"

"Come on, sis—you know I got you and I love spending time with my nephew."

"Thank you; I appreciate it and he loves spending time with his TT, as well."

"Good morning, Mr. Brooks—how was your morning run?"

"It was good, thanks; it wasn't too hot and there was a slight breeze. How is your day going so far?"

"It's been good so far. I have a doctor's appointment later today, so I'll be leaving a little early."

"Oh, ok, that's fine. Hey, can you tell Terrance that I need to talk to him as soon as he gets here?"

"Ok, I sure will."

"What's my morning looking like today?"

"It's slim this morning for some reason; you don't have anything until ten o'clock, you have a few things at eleven, and then you're done until one-thirty."

"Ok, thank you. I hope your doctor's appointment goes well. It's nothing serious, is it?"

"Oh no, just a checkup."

"Ok, well let me know if you need anything." "I will and thank you."

"No problem."

"Oh, hey T, I'm glad I ran into you—I need to talk to you; I'll walk you to your office."

"Ok, what up? This sounds urgent."

"You will never guess who I got a call from yesterday."

"I don't know, but someone has you excited—you look like you are about to ask somebody to prom or something."

"Jasmine called me last night and wants to meet with me to talk about something."

"Well, what did she say?"

"I just told you—she said that she wanted to talk and that it had to be in person. So, we agreed on the spot where we first met in the park."

"Why there?"

"I don't know; I'm assuming because it's a public place."

"Do you think it's about the case?"

"No, I don't think so; she could have done that over the phone. Besides, we aren't even close to negotiations or anything of that nature; the only thing I can think of is that she wants to talk about us."

"Really? Well, if that is the case, how do you feel about that and her?"

"I don't know; I mean, I still have feelings for her. At one point, she was everything that I ever wanted in a woman and potential wife. Now she has a kid, and we have this case against each other—not to mention there is this thing that I have going on with Marla. Even though we haven't defined anything yet, we have been seeing a lot of each other. I'm just not sure of how I feel about her; it's all so new and she is the first woman I've spent any time with since Jasmine."

"If there's one thing I know about you, it's that you will find a way to do what's best—you always have. Trust your gut and, more importantly, trust God. Pray about it and listen to his voice to guide you. Now, if I can offer my two cents: I love everything Marla has to offer; she is smart, wealthy, beautiful, and she can offer you some much. However, I've never seen you light up about anyone the way you did when you were with Jasmine. Even when you talk about her now, you have this smile—this glow—that you can't explain. I don't know if that means anything to you or not, but that's my two cents for what it's worth."

"Bro, you know I trust your judgement, and I know out of all the people in this world, you are the one person that has my best interests at heart. I appreciate that and you, my brother!"

"Hey, that's what family is for! Well, how about we get some work done? We have a lot to do."

"Yea, I guess you're right. What's your schedule looking like this morning?"

"I have a couple of status calls and a few motions, so not too much."

"Ok good; I was hoping both of us could be in court this afternoon for Ms. Henderson."

"Ok, no problem; I will make sure that I am done in enough time. I do have to meet with a client over the lunch break, though, so I will meet you at the courthouse."

"Ok, sounds good, T. I'll see you later then."

"Shay, come on down and get your breakfast before it gets cold."

"Coming, Momma. Why are you all dressed up, Momma?"

"I have court this afternoon at one-thirty and I have a few errands to run before that, so I'll be in and out all day."

"Ok. I'm going to go down to the community center and help, so if I'm not here that's where I will be. I wish I could go with you, though."

"I know, baby, but this is for the best. I don't want you anywhere near the courthouse with all these reporters around asking a million questions—it's best that you stay away, trust me. I trust Troy and Terrance, and I believe that everything will work out in our favor. We got this; you just handle your business in school."

"Ok, Momma. Just text me when you're done and let me know what happened."

"You know I will, baby. Now hurry up and eat so we can get going. You can take the car today; I'm going to call a driver and have him take me to the courthouse. I know parking will be crazy downtown, with all those reporters around shoving their cameras in my face."

"Hey, sis, good morning! I'm on my way there. I'm about a block away with Tre and it's been a crazy morning already. Tre threw up three times all over his clothes, so I've had to change him twice and as I'm changing him, I noticed a hole in my skirt so then I had to change—and now it seems like I've caught every red light from here to your house, and I know that pain in my butt coworker is looking at his watch right now, saying to himself that I'm late and it's because I have a baby.

"Hold on, sis. Treeee…"

"Hello, Jasmine? Your phone broke up. I can't hear you…Hello? Hello? Hello? Jasmine? Jasmine!"

Precious can hear the screeching of tires. "Jasmine, are you ok? What's going on, Jasmine? Jasmine? Jasmine…please answer me. Oh my God. Oh my God. Jasmine, are you alright? Please say something."

Precious can hear the sirens in the background as they grow closer to her, and she runs outside. The police and fire department arrive simultaneously. As she gets closer to the scene, she can see that's its Jasmine's t-boned car; the firefighters are working feverishly to get the doors open to the car. She can only see a glimpse of Jasmine and sees blood everywhere. She is now panicking.

"Let me through! That's my sister, that's my sister!

Let me through!"

"Ma'am, can we have a minute to get her out and into the ambulance, please?"

"Where is my nephew?"

"He is still in the car, ma'am; they are getting him out as well. Let us do our job and we will let you come through as soon as we are ready to transport them both. They have both lost a lot of blood, so we need to work as fast as we can and we cannot do that if they are trying to deal with you. I understand that you are scared and worried about your family. However, you must let us do what we do." The officer finishes talking to Precious as Jasmine and Tre are being rolled into the ambulance. Neither one of them is moving or appears to be conscious; Jasmine's face is bloody, and Tre's shirt is covered with blood. Precious is even more scared than before.

"Can I at least ride with them to the hospital?" Precious asks.

"Yes, get in—just remember to let them do their job."

"Hey, Clea, this is Precious. I was calling you to let you know Jasmine was in a car accident this morning. She is doing ok now, but they are running some tests on her just to be sure she is ok. Tre has some internal bleeding, and they are trying to figure out the extent of his injuries. I just wanted to let you know before you heard it somewhere else. I'm getting ready to go into Jasmine's room now; they just brought her up from getting x-rays. It's room 815."

"Ok, Precious; thanks for letting me know. I'm on my way now; I should be there in a few."

"Ok, I'll see you soon."

"Hey Jasmine, how are you feeling? You, ok?"

"Yes, I'm fine—just banged up with some sore ribs and a headache. Where is my baby? Why isn't he with you?"

"You don't remember? You never made it to my house. The accident was down the street from the house."

"No, wait—I did drop him off."

"No, you didn't, sis. You were in a serious accident. Tre is here in the hospital with some internal bleeding; I haven't been able to see him yet. I rode over here with you two in the ambulance—you were out of it the entire time."

"We have got to find my baby. Where is my baby?"

"Jasmine, calm down—let me get the nurse. I'll be right back, ok?"

"Good afternoon, Ms. Jones. How are you feeling?"

"I'm still a little sore and banged up with a slight headache, but other than that I'm fine. How is my baby? Where is he? I want to see my son!"

"Ok, well that's good. My name is Doctor William Davis and I've been taking care of your son. Right now, he is having some internal bleeding, and we are having a tough time stopping it. It looks like he may need surgery because he is losing so much blood. He may need a blood transfusion if we can't control the bleeding. If a transfusion is needed, do we have your permission to go ahead with that? And do you know how we can contact his father; in case your blood doesn't match then we can see if his blood is a match?"

"I know our blood types don't match because he had jaundice when he was a born and the doctors told me it was because our blood types don't match."

"Ok, well that's good to know. How can we reach his father, then?"

"I don't know; I haven't seen him in quite some time now. I'll have to try to make some calls. In the meantime, can I see my baby now?"

"Yes, you can see him—just don't get him too excited; we need to keep him as still as possible. He is still a little sedated, as well, in order to keep him that way. I'll let you get settled; I'm sure they will want to keep you under observation for at least the rest of the day. As soon as you get information on the dad, please contact me at once."

"I will, Dr. Davis, and thank you for taking care of my baby."

"No problem, Ms. Jones."

"I think I might have a business card or something; he had a side business because he was in school. Can you pass me my purse? I've got so much stuff in here; I need to clean it out. Here it is! I had forgotten all about it. Delvin Rashad, aka DJ Spank…oh my God, what was I thinking? Well, here goes nothing."

"Hello, may I speak to Mr. Rashad, please?" "This is him."

"Hey, Delvin, this is Jasmine Jones. We met about a year and a half ago at Club A."

"Ok, yea, I remember you. How have you been? I did not think I would ever hear from you again, since you said what we did was a mistake."

"Well, I was in a bad place at that time, and you said you understood."

"I did; I'm not upset or anything. We both were two adults having a fun time and to be honest, I wasn't in a good place at that time either, so it is what it is. Why are you calling now, though?"

"I need to talk to you and it's important."

"Ok, go ahead; I've got some time before my shift starts."

"I was hoping to talk to you in person—like I said, it's important."

"Ok, where do you want to meet?"

"Well, I'm not sure if you heard or not on the news, but I'm in the hospital. I was in a bad accident this morning."

"Oh wow. Are you ok?"

"Yes, I'm fine. I'm at North Hospital, right off Highway 4, in room 815."

"Ok, well, I am going that way for work, so I can stop by."

"Ok great; I'll see you in a few." "Ok, thanks. Bye."

"What did he say, sis?" Precious asks.

"He said he would stop by on his way to work and that he would be here in a few minutes."

"What are you going to tell him?"

"I'm going to tell him the truth—that he has a baby that needs him. What choice do I have?"

"Yes, I guess you're right. Do you want me to leave so you can have some privacy?" There's a knock at the door.

"Hello, Jasmine; I'm here. What is so important that we need to talk about?"

"Excuse me—I am going to step outside and let you two have a conversation. I'll be in the waiting room, sis," Precious says.

"Ok, can you close the door? Close the door!" "Jasmine, what is going on? I haven't seen or heard from you and now you want to talk? I'm going back to work," Delvin says.

"Oh, wait a minute—you work here? I didn't know that."

"Yes, I work here. I do the blood draws here for the hospital. Remember when I told you that I was going to school? This is what I was going to school for; I did my internship here and they hired me once I finished. Can we get back to why you called, please?"

"Well, there is no straightforward way to tell you this, but after that night we were together, I got pregnant and had your son."

"What?! You had my son? You are tripping now."

"No, Delvin, really—I had your son. You're the only guy I have been with."

"Wait, you were living with some guy from what I can remember. How do you know it's not his baby?"

"Because at that time, he and I had not been intimate—we were more like roommates than anything else. Now, the reason I called you is because our son may need a blood transfusion. The doctors are saying that he has some internal bleeding and that they are struggling to get it stopped. It might be his spleen or something at this point; I'm not sure—all I know is that it is very serious. I know my blood doesn't match his, so the doctors said that I should call his father, which is why I called you. Our son needs you. I understand you may be mad at me and that I'm throwing a lot at you right now, but Tre needs you!"

"Whoa, wait a minute, Jasmine. Let me sit down for a second. You're telling me that I have a son and his life may be in danger! Wow! This is crazy! Let me ask you this? If you hadn't gotten into this accident, would you have told me?"

"That's a good question—and to be honest I don't know. I mean, it's been on my mind a lot lately to reach out and to explain things to you, I just didn't know how. I felt so bad about what happened that I didn't know what to do. I was in love with my boyfriend, and he didn't know what he wanted, and I just felt alone. Then we had drinks and one thing led to another and before you know it, we had slept together. That's not me—I'm not some random chick who does that. I had plans; I have a career that is flourishing; I was completing my goals and now I have a baby. It was a lot for me, too, and I didn't want to bring you into all of that if that makes sense. I know it may sound selfish and all, but I am the first in my family to go to school and have a good paying job; I was breaking generational curses that have plagued my family for years and years. I felt as though having a baby out of wedlock would have set us back again; I felt like I had let the family down and that was too much to bear. Now my baby needs me to step up and do the right thing—my baby needs his father to save his life. Would you please get tested and save our child?"

"Yes, I'll get myself tested but we have a lot to talk about. I've already missed about a year or so, thanks to you! I'm not doing this for you, I'm doing this for him. I need to get going, and I'll get this taken care of. Since I work in the lab, we can get this done right away and get him whatever he needs. I'll see you later. I'm assuming it's Tre Jones, right?"

"Yes, that's right and thank you—thank you so much for doing this."

"Yea ok; I'll talk to you later."

"Girl, how did it go? He didn't look happy walking out of here," Precious asks as she comes back into the room.

"He wasn't," Jasmine replies.

There's a knock, and Clea walks in the hospital room.

"Hey Jasmine, how are you doing?"

"Hey Clea, how did you know I was here?" "Precious called me."

"I'm good; just worried about Tre." "Well, is there anything I can do?" "No, just pray for my baby."

"I already did that!" Clea replies. "I know."

"Who was that guy that just walked out?" "Girl, that was Tre's father."

"Huh? Wait a minute—you two have been talking and you didn't tell me?"

"No, this was the first time I had seen him since that night I got pregnant. Tre has some internal bleeding and may need a blood transfusion from him—I had no choice but to call him and see if he could donate blood."

"Oh ok. Well, how did he take the news of being a father?"

"He took it better than I thought he would. I could tell he was upset and hurt that he has had a son all this time and I didn't tell him, not to mention when he finally hears the news it's a do or die situation. He said he would help him and donate blood, though. I'm glad he didn't do the whole 'that isn't my baby' garbage like some men—you know how they do."

"You know, sis, I would have been on that head had he pulled that mess. I was right outside wishing he would clown or say something stupid!" Precious says.

"Precious, stop! Can someone take me upstairs so I can see my baby, please? I'm still a little weak."

"Hold on Jasmine, I'll get you a wheelchair so you can stay off your feet."

"Thanks, Clea."

"Man T, I can't believe Ms. Henderson didn't show up for court today. You don't think she is trying to run, do you?"

"Man, I don't know what to think—I thought we had convinced her that we had a good case, not to mention she knows how much money Marla put up for her bail. The judge is going to revoke her bond if we don't find her soon and throw her right back in jail—and this time, it won't be a bond. Tori, can you step into my office please?"

"Yes Mr. Brooks. What can I do for you?"

"Can you call Ms. Henderson's home phone and cell phone, and see if she answers? She missed court today and we have twenty-four hours to produce her or else the judge is going to issue a bench warrant for her arrest."

"Ok, I'll do that right now." "Thank you."

"Mr. Brooks; Mr. Mays; you should turn on the TV in your office. Ms. Henderson was in a car accident with Ms. Jones."

"Are you serious?"

"Yes, I'm reading the ticker at the bottom, and it said that Assistant State Attorney Jasmine Jones was in a car accident with Patricia Henderson, who is the suspect in the murder of Senator Johnson. All the parties involved in the crash were taken to the hospital, including a young child under the age of two.”

“Oh my God—Jasmine and the baby. T, you have to take me to the hospital now!”

“Troy calm down…we can go—just don’t forget that Patricia is our client and that’s our priority.”

“Hello, Ms. Henderson; it’s Troy and Terrance— may we come in? How are you feeling?”

“Well right now I feel good; they have me on some good pain medication. I must have hit my head on the window in the back seat. The doctor said I have a concussion. I blacked out so I don’t remember much of the accident; I’m just tired.”

“Oh, ok. Well, we can go and let you get your rest— we just wanted to check on you. Do you need anything?”

“No, I’m fine. Can one of you call my daughter and let her know that I was in an accident and that I’m ok and here in the hospital? Do you know if the driver who was driving me is ok? And the other people in the other car?”

“Your driver is ok; he just had some bumps and bruises. We are not sure about the other people; we will check on them though. You get some rest, and we will check on you in the morning. I’ll also have my secretary get your daughter and bring her to you.”

“Oh, thank you so much. She worries about me like she is the momma and I’m the daughter.”

“Well, that just means you raised her right. Have a good night.”

“Excuse me nurse, can you tell me which room Jasmine Jones is in?”

"Oh yeah, she is right down the hall in room 815."
"Thank you very much."

"You're welcome."

"Troy, what are you doing?" Terrance asks.

"I should go check on her, T. We may be going against each other in the courtroom, but I still care about her. I just want to see if she is ok, that's it."

"Ok, man. I'll wait for you in the waiting room." "Ok. I won't be long."

Troy knocks on the door of room 815 and quietly peeks in. "Hey, Jasmine, do you mind if I come in?"

"Sure, come on in."

"I didn't see you ladies over there; I hope I'm not interrupting."

"No, you're not interrupting, we were just talking. In fact, we will leave you two alone and go grab some coffee or something. Can we get you something?"

"No, I'm good, thank you," Troy answers, then turns his focus to Jasmine. "How are you doing?"

"I'm making it. How about you?" "I'm doing alright."

"What brings you here?"

"I heard about your accident, and I had to see if you were ok. I mean, I wanted to come check in on you and see if you were ok."

"I'm ok, but my son Tre isn't doing well." Jasmine's eyes begin to tear up and her voice is now trembling; her hands are visibly shaking. "Tre has some internal bleeding and may need a blood transfusion if they can't stop the bleeding."

Troy moves in closer to console her giving her a hug. Jasmine buries her head in his chest. "I know he will be fine," Troy tries to reassure her. "If there is anything I can do, I'm just a phone call away. You know that right?"

"I know, Troy. I'm sorry; I didn't mean to break down like that."

"No, no—don't be silly; I understand. If there is anyone who understands the bond between a mother and her son, it's me—you don't have to apologize. You also don't have to be strong all the time; there are a lot of people around here who love and care for you who will do whatever it takes to make sure you're ok."

"Thank you, Troy, I appreciate you saying that. Are you one of those people?"

"I guess I am. I mean, I am here right now." "True, you are here and I'm glad to see you."

"I don't want to wear out my welcome; I'm sure your family wants to come in and see you. If you need anything, please don't hesitate to call or text me. I'll be praying for you all." They embrace once again and Troy hugs her a little tighter then kisses her on the forehead. "Take care, Jasmine."

"You do the same. Talk to you later."

As Troy is walking out, Precious and Clea are walking back into the room.

"Girl, what was that all about," Precious asks. "He was just checking on me to see if I was ok."

"No, that look on your face says that it was more than that."

"No really, Troy is a sweet guy. He wanted to let me know that if I needed anything that I could call on him—that's it."

"No, Jasmine, there was more to it than that. We saw you two hugging—and that kiss on the forehead also said it was more than just him checking on you. That man still loves and cares about you; you could see it in his face that he still has feelings for you."

"I don't know about all that! Right now, I need to focus on Tre. My relationship with Troy has sailed, and I have accepted that."

Delvin burst into the room and throws the lab paperwork on Jasmine's bed. "Why are you playing these mind games with me? First, you told me that I'm a father and you didn't know how to tell me! Then, you say that our son is hurt and needs a blood transfusion and that you're not a match so then I must be the father. Now come to find out, I'm not the father—our blood types are 99.9 percent not compatible. How could you do this to me?"

"Wait what? What are you talking about?" Jasmine grabs the papers from her bed and begins to scan them over. "I don't understand; you have to be the father."

"Well, you can read it for yourself—I'm not a match. We did the test three times and each time it said the same damn thing. I am not the father. What kind of woman does this to someone?"

"Hey, wait a minute—back off. You're doing too much. Her son is fighting for his life and needs help," Precious says.

"No, stop, sis—I got this. Listen Delvin, I didn't mean for any of this to happen; I had no plans of getting pregnant and I didn't plan to hide anything from you, nor did I plan to have an accident that would land us here. I'm sorry that I didn't tell you sooner that I was pregnant and that it could be yours. But what you're not going to do is come in here and act like I'm some random chick trying to pin a baby off on someone. Let's be clear: I don't need you or your money. My baby is in need, so I reached out to who I thought was his father. You and Troy are the only men that I have been with."

"Man, whatever. I am not trying to hear none of that—I see this all the time. Women putting their children off on other men, claiming they're the daddy—this is how women get hurt out here, playing these games."

"Wait a minute, what is that supposed to mean?"

"Nothing, I'm just saying—women use their children all the time to either back at their man or they use them as pawns to get a man!"

"Now, see, that's where you got me messed up—I don't need a man for nothing. I have my own and can do it on my own. Besides, I don't want you! Let's get that clear. I didn't tell you about Tre to try to get you in my life or the life of my son; we would have been good without you and will continue to be good without you."

"Mr. Delvin, is it? I would suggest you get out of my sister's room or we are going to have some problems."

Precious and Clea both stand up between Jasmine and Delvin.

"Yea, ok. It's time for me to get back to work anyways."

Jasmine's eyes are now flowing with tears. She is saddened yet happy to know that Delvin is not Tre's father. She now realizes that she must go through this all over again with Troy and how hurt he will be to just now find out that Tre is his son, and that he has missed all these moments of his life.

"Sister, I got to tell you—I'm glad that he is not my nephew's dad. What did you see in him, anyway?"

"Well at the time, it must have been the alcohol. How am I going to tell Troy, though? What am I going to do now?"

"You're going to get yourself together, put your big girl pants on, and do what's best for your son. Whatever happens, we will take this one step at a time—no matter what, we got you and will be here for you and Tre. Remember: you're Jasmine Jones and you do this every day. You have taken down murderers, drug dealers, and all kinds of different people. You're a strong, fierce, and independent woman. You got this."

"Yea, your right."

"Troy, how did it go with you and Jasmine? Is she ok?"

"Yes, she is fine; however, her son is fighting for his life right now. He has some internal bleeding that they are having trouble stopping and he may need a blood transfusion—to save his life."

"Oh wow. Is there anything we can do to help? What do you think about setting up a blood drive right here at the office?"

"That's a great idea, T. Can you head that up for me?"

"Man, you know I got you. Now give me the real and none of this surface stuff—how was it to see Jasmine again?"

"On the real, bro? It felt good. Even though it was under terrible circumstances, it felt like old times. At one point when she was crying and telling me about what had happened, all I wanted to do was comfort her and make her feel safe in my arms; when I gave her a hug it was like she just melted in my chest. At that exact moment, everything was alright with the world."

"You see? That right there—that look you just had. My brother, you still love that woman. It's time you stop denying yourself and be happy."

"I'm not."

"Yes, you are, Troy. You are and you know I'm right— there is nothing in this world that you wouldn't do for that woman if she asked you. Life happened and things got out of control the first time you were together, and this may be your second chance at love—a true love at that. Love like this doesn't come along too often, let alone twice, and here it is looking at you dead in the face."

"I hear you, Terrance, I do; but what about Marla, man? She is a good girl, too!"

"That is true, but she doesn't make you feel like Jasmine does. All I'm saying is give it some time; don't rush into anything with Marla and have an open mind when it comes to Jasmine. You don't have to decide right now, and nobody is asking anybody to get married or anything like that right— unless I'm missing something. And didn't you have some reservations when it came to Marla? And you guys are not exclusive, are you? If not, then what's wrong with seeing if you and Jasmine could build a future together?"

"I hear you; I really do. Jasmine has a kid and I'm not sure if I'm ready to be a stepfather or a father. Life is good; I can come and go as I please without the worry of finding a babysitter. I can do anything I want on my own time without hesitation. I'm not saying that I don't want kids or anything—I just don't know; it's a lot of responsibility to raise kids. Hell, I'm a mess myself. I'm still trying to get right and I don't want her kid to possibly be messed up in the head like me with all these hidden feelings and not knowing how to deal with them."

"Troy, isn't that why you're getting help? Look, we all have messed up and needed help. You are doing something about it by getting help. I wish more people had the nerve to seek help, and that includes myself. It takes a lot of courage to admit that you need help and I admire that about you—you're not afraid to admit it. The world would be a much better place if men would seek help. If the senator had gotten help, he would still be alive today. Look at how many people suffer from domestic violence daily, but men and women, and they don't tell anybody. If men knew how to properly express themselves, the world would be so different."

"I'll take your advice—enough of all that though. Can we get a motion on file at once to explain to the judge why he shouldn't hold Patricia in criminal contempt of court for not showing up at today's court date?"

"That's already taken care of. While you were talking with Jasmine, I called the office and told my secretary Karen to draft and file the motion for us. We are back in court tomorrow morning at nine o'clock."

"Ok cool, thanks T. Now, enough about me, what's going on in your world? We always talk about what's going on in my life."

"Nothing much, everything is going well. I'm still kind of seeing Marla's friend from that one night. I'm not sure where it's going yet; however, we are having fun. She is planning a little weekend getaway next month. She won't tell me where we are going, though—she wants to surprise me. I'm sure it will be nice, though. So far, I've learned that when she does something, she goes all out and is incredibly detailed like me—which is a good thing. I really like that about her."

"Yea, you need someone like that. Remember that one girl you were dating, the free spirit? I know that drove you nuts."

"Oh my God, I couldn't stand that. I understand being spontaneous and all, but man—as busy as I am, I can't always just fly by the seat of my pants."

"I get it…hold on, T—this is Jasmine calling me." "Hey Jasmine, is everything ok?"

"No, it's not! I really need to talk to you; it's important!"

"What's going on?"

"I don't want to talk over the phone. Can you please come back to the hospital?"

"Yes, of course I can. I'll be right there!" "Thank you, I'll see you soon."

"Ok."

"What was that about?" Terrance asks.

"I don't know; she wouldn't tell me. She just said that she wanted to talk to me about something important in person. She wants me to come to her hospital room."

"That's weird, I wonder why she wouldn't at least tell you what it's about."

"I don't know, T; I'll find out when I get there." "Ok, I'll finish here at the office."

"Ok cool, thanks, man. I'll call you later and let you know what's going on."

"Ok, let me know if you need anything." "Hey Jasmine, can I come in?"

"REVEALED"

"Yes, come on in." Troy walks into the room. He could see Jasmine had been crying; her eyes are all red and a little puffy. As he gets closer to the bed, he reaches for her hand.

"What's up? What's going on? I could tell something was wrong. Are you ok? Is Tre ok?"

"Yes, I'm fine. However, Tre is not. As I told you, he is having some complications from the accident. He has some internal bleeding and needs a blood transfusion. When he was born, Tre had jaundice, so I know that my blood is not a match—that means his father would be the next person in line to be a match for him. Earlier today, you said that you would do whatever you could to help us. I…or we…would like you to have your blood tested to see if you're a match for him."

"Wait…huh. I'm not understanding…why would my blood type be a match for him? Shouldn't you be going to his father? Do you want me to find him and let him know?"

"No, Troy; please sit down. When your mother was ill and eventually passed, I wanted to be there for you so badly, and every time I tried, you pushed me away or shut me out altogether—for months I felt like I was in a relationship all by myself. I know you had a lot going on at the time, so I tried to be understanding. However, I felt all alone, like I was your roommate rather than your girlfriend. We were barely intimate with one another. We were like two ship's passing in the night. At night, I silently cried myself to sleep on the couch while you slept in the bed. You were completely oblivious as to what was going on in our relationship. I longed to have a piece of you; anything that I could hold on too that would give me hope, or a sign that things would eventually go back to normal, and that day never came. That night that I went out, I felt so broken inside."

"Jasmine, stop. You don't have to say anything or apologize, or any of that—I know that I drove you away and for that I am terribly sorry. I didn't know how to manage it. I was a mess, and I can say that now. I take full responsibility for my actions, and I apologize for treating you the way that I did. You didn't deserve that."

"Thank you, Troy, that means a lot to me. It also helps me with why I called you to come back. Troy, the reason Tre needs you to get your blood tested is to see if you're a match…because the other guy who I presumed to be the father was tested, and it turns out that he is not the father. Troy, you're Tre's father! I am so sorry that you had to find out this way; I really am. However, Tre is fighting for his life and is in need. I understand if you hate me and never want to lay eyes on me ever again—just don't take it out on him, please. I am begging you."

Jasmine gets out of bed and walks over to Troy. He slides down in his chair with his hands buried in his face; the pain and hurt is showing all over his body language. A tear rolls slowly down his cheek.

"Say something, Troy—please."

"I honestly don't know what to say; this is a lot to take in. Wow, I could be a father? Why didn't you tell me sooner?"

"I didn't know how to tell you, and I just assumed because we weren't really sleeping with one another that it wasn't your baby. I knew I had already hurt you by having the one-night stand; I didn't want to add any more to it. I always hoped and wished that you were the father, but I was too afraid and to hurt to allow myself to even dream of that being a reality. Now that this is happening, I really have no choice. I hate to even ask you this; however, Tre needs you— and to be honest, I need you, too. You were the best thing that had ever happened to me along with having Tre. Would you please consider getting tested?"

Troy takes a deep breath, and sighs then pauses briefly. "Yes, of course I will get tested."

Jasmine jumps into his arms and squeezes him. Troy wraps his arms around her and hugs her so tight, as if he were reassuring her that he has her back. Jasmine kisses Troy on the check and thanks him. "Come with me, Troy; I want you to see him."

"Oh wow…he looks so peaceful laying there. I would never know he's hurting or that anything is wrong with him. Do you really think he could be our son…my son?"

"Yes, Troy. I was only with one other guy besides you, and we know he is not the father."

"You know what's crazy? That day I saw you both in the park—I thought he looked familiar, like I had seen him somewhere before. I just could not place where."

"I saw the same thing that day. Then when I got home, I saw this birth mark on his arm, and it instantly reminded me of your mommas' birthmark. He is such a sweet and loving little boy; he's a happy baby. Once you get to know him, you will fall in love with him."

"Whoa, let's slow down a little bit—this is all happening so fast."

"Here comes Dr. Davis."

"Hello sir, I'm Doctor William Davis; I'm Tre's doctor."

"I'm Troy Brooks, nice to meet you."

"Well, I'm sure by now Jasmine has told you what's going on with Tre's conditions."

"Yes, she has. Once I take the test, how soon will we know the results?"

"We will put a rush on it and if all goes well, we could do the procedure tomorrow if needed—if that's OK with you."

"Yes, Doc, that will be fine. Thank you for taking care of him."

"No problem at all. I'll contact you as soon as we find out the results of your test. If you don't mind, sir, can I get you to go down to the second floor? That's where our lab technicians are who will be taking your blood to test."

"I'm on my way, Doc."

"Troy, do you want me to go with you?"

"No, you can stay up here with Tre; I need some time to collect my thoughts."

"Ok, I understand." Jasmine grabs him, hugs him, and kisses him lightly on the lips. Troy is all messed up on the inside; his thoughts are everywhere. What if this was his son? What does that mean for him and Jasmine? Is he ready to be a dad? Will Tre be ok even after the transfusion? How will this change his life? This changes everything! What am I going to do?

Troy takes out his phone and sends a text to Terrance and Mike. "Fellas, I really need to talk to you tonight in person. Some things have happened, and I really need your help and input. I'll call you when I leave the hospital and I'm headed home."

"Mr. Brooks, we are ready for you to come back now. You can take your jacket off and hang it up there and roll up one sleeve to your elbow. Now, just relax and I'll be as gentle as possible."

Troy clears his throat. "Do you know how long it will take to assess my blood to see if I am compatible to do a blood transfusion?"

"It doesn't take too long; we are going to put a rush on it so a couple of hours at the most. That's a wonderful thing you're doing for someone; I'm sure they really appreciate it. All done. Can you hold this right here while I get you a band aid? Thank you, sir. You're all set."

"No, thank you. So, how will I know if I am a match?"

"We will give you a call or email you as soon as we get them back."

"Ok great, thanks again. Take care."

Troy heads back up to where Tre is being treated by the doctors and sees Jasmine sitting next to his bed.

"Hey, all done. Now we just wait. Have you eaten anything or had anything to drink?"

"No, I'm fine. I can't eat or drink anything right now, anyway. I feel like this is all my fault, like I'm being punished for sleeping with Delvin; for not telling you that I was pregnant; that I was pregnant and had a baby. I'm sorry for all this mess! It's all my fault!"

"No, Jasmine—you can't think like that. It doesn't do you or Tre any good. Right now, he needs you to be positive and strong. He's a fighter just like his mom, and I'm sure he is going to pull through this with no lasting effects. He will be running around playing catch, playing with bugs, and getting on your nerves in no time."

"Playing with bugs…ewe, who does that?"

"I did; if he's anything like me, he will be playing with bugs." They both chuckle. Troy, not realizing what he just said, sees Jasmine looking at him with those beautiful brown eyes.

"I sure hope so—I hope he is just like you. It was a mistake leaving you like I did. It was a huge mistake and one that I regret."

"One of my biggest regrets is shutting you out. If I hadn't pushed you away, you would never have felt the need to go out that night. You are the greatest love that I have ever known. You are everything that I ever wanted and everything I didn't even know I wanted—I was just too dumb to appreciate what I had in front of me."

Jasmine gently grabs Troy by the face and kisses him like two estranged lovers meeting each other after months of being apart.

"Excuse me, I am looking for Ms. Jones and Mr.

Brooks?"

"That would be us."

"Here are the lab results for you, Mr. Brooks. Your office told us that you were here."

"I'm sorry, I must have given you the wrong number mistakenly."

"It's no problem, sir. Here you go."

"I don't think I've ever been this anxious and nervous about anything—let's read it together."

Troy's hands are shaking and sweating as he pulls out the results.

"Well, what does it say, Troy?"

"I can't believe it! I can't believe it! I'm a dad; Tre is my son!" Jasmine throws her arms around Troy again. "It's

99.9 percent that I am his dad." Tears begin to flow from both of their eyes.

"I don't know what to say—I'm speechless," Troy says. "When and how do we schedule the transfusion?"

"Well, Dr. Davis did say that if the bleeding stopped, Tre would not need it. We should just pray that the bleeding will stop, and that God continues to cover our baby." Jasmine explains to Troy.

Troy and Jasmine grab hands with each other and Tre, as Troy begins to pray.

"Father, thank you that you always hear me. Father, I come right now asking that you continue to cover our son, Tre. We pray that you heal his body and keep him covered; allow him to grow up and become the man of God that you have called him to be; allow him to be a leader and not a follower of men. Father, we pray that you keep him safe from all hurt, harm, and danger, seen and unseen—let him be a light to others as you are the light to us. Father, we pray right now for his mother and his father, that they make the right decisions when it comes to Tre. Let them be on one accord in all things that concern him. We ask all these things in your son's Jesus' name, Amen."

Troy leans over and kisses his son on the forehead. "Thank you, Troy, for that prayer," Jasmine says.

"You don't have to thank me—he's our son and I will always pray for him and with him. I want to be everything for him that I didn't have. I don't ever want him to go without or be lacking like I did."

"I'm sure he won't—we have a lot to talk about."

"Yea, I guess we do. Let's do that later, though. Right now, let's just love on Tre until he gets better—we can figure the rest out later."

"I agree!" Troy and Jasmine spend the rest of the night talking about Tre until they both fall asleep in Tre's room.

OUT IN THE OPEN

"Clerk, call the next case."

"Case number 22CF4237; the people of the state of Illinois versus Patricia Henderson."

"Good morning, Mr. Wiley and Mr. Mays. I see your client is still not present, and by the looks of it neither is Mr. Brooks. Do you care to explain? It is your motion."

"Well, your honor—if we could pass this case for just a moment, I'm sure Mr. Brooks will be here; it would be just a few minutes."

"Ok, we will pass this case for just a few minutes and when I return, I expect to see council and your client. Court is in recess."

Terrance hurries out the courtroom to call Troy. "Hello?"

"Hello."

"Troy!"

"Hey, what's up, T?"

"Bro, I know you are not still asleep. Did you forget we had court at nine this morning?"

"Oh my God, yes, I did! I'm so sorry. I'm on my way right now."

Jasmine wakes up. "We had court this morning and I'm late; I'll talk to you later. Keep me informed about what's going on," Troy tells her. Troy runs out of the room and dashes out of the hospital. He doesn't have time to go home and change, so he heads straight to the courthouse and sees Terrance waiting in front of the courtroom.

"Troy, what's going on, man? You are never late and what's worse—you still have on the same clothes from yesterday."

"I know; a lot has happened in the last twelve hours or so. I'll fill you in later. What was Judge Walkers mood when he got off the bench?"

"He was not happy!"

"Ok, well, he will understand. Come on—let's go back in and I'll explain everything to you later."

"Bailiff, can you let Judge Walker know we are ready?"

"Yes, I'll get him right now."

"Please remain seated—court is now in session; the honorable Judge Anthony Walker presiding. I see Mr. Brooks has decided to join us now. Good morning, Mr. Brooks."

"Good morning, sir, and I apologize for being late." "Where is your client, Mr. Brooks?"

"Your honor, our client was in a bad car accident yesterday and may have a concussion—that's why she isn't here. The doctors are keeping her for observation for a day or two. If you go back and look at her record, you will see that she has never missed a court date. Furthermore, your honor, today was just set for a status on discovery."

"Your honor, state's attorney Alvin Wiley for the people. I'll be taking over this case along with attorney Jasmine Jones, who was also in the accident that involved Ms. Henderson. I would like to turn over everything we have to Mr. Brooks for this case."

"Your honor, I acknowledge receipt of the state's evidence. Thank you, Mr. Wiley."

"Your honor, we have also extended an offer to Mr.

Brooks and his client for their consideration."

"Yes, they have, your honor, and I will discuss it with my client. Can we come back in about thirty days to see where we are?"

"Your honor, we have also filed a motion for a speedy trial."

"No objection, your honor."

"So, thirty days puts us around July 10th at one- thirty; let's make sure everyone is here on time and ready to go. Madam clerk, call the next case."

"Troy, now, what happened? Last I heard from you was that text you sent to me and Mike saying you wanted to talk," Terrance asks.

"Man, T; I don't even know where to start—so much has happened in the last twelve hours, bro. My world has been flipped, shaken, and everything else. As you know, Jasmine called me back to the hospital, right? When I got there, we started talking and she apologized for the breakup, sleeping with that guy, and leaving me, right? I in turn acknowledged my role in the breakup and told her that I was sorry for my part in it all. She then continues to tell me about her son and how he got hurt in the accident and was bleeding internally; if they couldn't get it to stop, he would need a blood transfusion. Well, Jasmine couldn't do it because they have two different blood types. So, according to the doctor, the next best donor would be the father. I'm like, ok…so, do you want me to help find the father? Is that why you called me? She was like no! I think you might be the father!"

"What?! Are you serious? Troy, stop playing with me. You're serious!"

"T, I am so serious. My mouth dropped when I heard that. I didn't know what to say or do—I was straight speechless!"

"I bet."

"She then goes on to tell me that she wishes things would have turned out differently between us, and that I was the best thing she ever had."

"What did you say?"

"T, I can't front—I told her she was the best thing that ever happened to me, too. Then we kissed—and man, I so missed the way she kisses me; it just made me forget everything. I know now that this might be the second chance you were telling me about. After the kiss, I went down and took the blood test and T…your boy is a daddy! Can you believe that I am somebody's father, bro?! Tre is my son! After we found out the results, we just talked the rest of the night like old times. Now, we are just waiting to see if Tre is going to need the transfusion or not."

"Man, this is crazy. I can't even imagine, Troy. Now, the big question is how you feel about all of this and the fact that you have a son—I've never heard you talk about having kids of your own."

"At first, I was shocked and didn't know how I felt. Then the more I looked at my baby boy…I don't know. It's like something came over me and I instantly fell in love with that kid. He has big brown eyes like my mom—he looks like my mom. I knew right then that I would do anything possible to keep him safe and protected. He is a perfect little angel."

"If you're happy, I'm happy, man. Congratulations; you deserve it. Now, the even bigger question is what's going on with you and Jasmine?"

"Well, we never talked about us after we found out that Tre is my son. I mean, I do love her and always will. After my mother, she is the only woman that I can honestly say that I have ever loved. She checks all the boxes for me— so, I really don't know."

"Well, you are forgetting one major thing." "What's that?"

"Did you forget about Marla Bordeaux?"

"Oh, snap—I did forget about that. We had dinner plans and I forgot to return her calls. I know she was probably blowing my phone up." Troy looks at his phone. "Yep, look at these sixty missed calls and texts."

"I'm sure she was worried about you."

"Yea, I'm sure she was. What am I going to tell her? Jasmine and her already don't like each other from their college days; they're not going to like each other now. Back in the day, they were best friends and roommates in college, then the two of them got into it about some guy Jasmine was dating and that Marla may have wanted and fooled around with. Here we are years later, and they haven't spoken to one another since."

"Man, that's crazy—and now it's happening all over again with you."

"Well technically, I'm not in a relationship with either one of them. Jasmine and I are not together, and Marla and I are not exclusive—neither one can be mad at the other concerning me. Marla is cool and all, but I'm in love with Jasmine. She has my heart and now my son!"

"Sounds like you have made up your mind, then—you're going to work things out with Jasmine."

"I hope so, bro. I really want to have a family, you know; something I never really had. I want to be there for them both."

"If that's what you want, you know I have your

back."

"Thanks T!"

"One last thing though—and I'm just looking at both sides of the coin as your friend—I must ask you: What if Jasmine doesn't want that? Do you really want Jasmine or do you just like the idea of having a family because you didn't have one growing up?"

"That's a valid question, and from the way it sounded last might, I think we both want to get back with each other. The way she kissed me…I could feel that love again; it is stronger than ever. Even if we didn't share a child, Jasmine was and is the love of my life. I was stupid to let her get away the first time and now if there is a second chance for us, I'm going to grab it. She is my one true soul mate, and we were made just for each other; she is the ribs that covers my heart. I absolutely love her, T!"

"Dang man, I can tell. That's all I need to hear. I am happy for you all, bro, and I got a little nephew, huh?"

"Yea man, and I can't wait for you to meet him. Oh, yea—let me call Mike and tell him too before I forget. Are you going back to the office?"

"Yea, I am. Why, what's up?"

"Nothing, just let Karen know that I'll be in after I go home and change then run back out to the hospital. Can you cover the few cases that I have today?"

"Yea I got you—go be with your son, Dad!" "Hey, sis. Good morning!" Precious says.

"Hey, what happened to you and Clea last night? You both just disappeared."

"Well, we knew you and Troy had a lot to talk about. So, are you going to tell me what happened or not? I thought you would have called me last night to tell me something."

"Well sis, Troy is the father!" Jasmine says in her Maury voice.

Precious screams with joy. "Are you serious?"

"Yes, girl—I'm dead serious. Troy Brooks is 99.9 percent Tre's father!"

"That's awesome! How did he take it?"

"He was shaken at first; he didn't know what to say but then he embraced it. He was excited about being a father. Then, to top it off, we kissed and talked all night about Tre until we fell asleep."

"Wait, what?! You kissed? How did that happen?"

"Girl, I don't even remember how exactly it happened; all I know is that we were talking, and one thing led to another and the next thing I know, we were kissing. He said he was sorry that things turned out like they did, and I apologized for this situation. Everything just seemed like it was coming together, and maybe—just maybe—Troy and I can work this out and become the family that I have secretly hoped we could."

"Sis, I'm so happy for you. I pray things work out for you. How's Tre doing this morning?"

"Things are looking brighter. The doctors left right before you came in and said that his vitals were looking better, and they think the bleeding has stopped. They are going to run some more tests to be sure, but so far things are looking good."

"Praise God…look at God work!"

"I know that's right, sis—say it again!" "What's next?"

"If he keeps improving, they're going to let us go home either later today or tomorrow morning; I should be released from here this afternoon."

"What about you and Troy?"

"Yea…that part. I'm not sure. I mean, things were great last night but there was a lot going on with him just finding out he was the father. Now that he has had some time to think over everything and grasp it all, I pray that he still feels the same way."

Just then, they are interrupted by Troy knocking on the door. "Hey Jasmine; Precious. How are you both?"

"We're good, thank you—and congrats, Dad!" Precious says. "How does it feel?"

"Well, to be honest, I'm still a little overwhelmed and trying to wrap my head around it all. However, I'm happy, excited, nervous, and worried…man, it's so many things running through my head right now."

"I'm sure you're going to be a great dad and both of you will make great parents to my nephew. I got to go and take care of some things. Jasmine, I'll be back to pick you guys up in a little while."

"Jasmine, I was hoping I could take you both home if that's ok. I would like to spend as much time as I can with you."

"I don't know, Troy. Don't get me wrong, I would love for you to take us home and be there with us; however, we still have this trial going and my boss and Alvin are already tripping about our past relationship. They are really going to flip out now that we have a child in common, and if they knew we were spending time together…oh my God. Alvin would have a conniption and try his best to get me off this case; it's going to be bad enough that I haven't been there in a couple of days—not to mention all the paparazzi that's covering our every move; this would be all over the news. How do you keep away from them?"

"Well, I do know my way around and how to get away from these crazy reporters and their cameras. I understand that this is going to be a tricky situation for you at work; I just want to be there for you."

"If you two will excuse me, I'll let you talk in private. Just call me and let me know your plans; I can come back to get you or just meet you at the house—either way is good for me. Troy, it was good to see you again. I hope we will see more of you now," Precious says.

"Oh, you will. So Ms. Jones, did I hear that correctly?

That you and Tre will be able to go home today?" "Yes, you did, Mr. Brooks."

"Does that mean that Tre doesn't need the transfusion?"

"Yes, that's what that means. Our baby is going to be ok! He's going to be fine."

"Oh wow…praise God! I was so worried about him."

"Yea, me too. The doctor said that they if they didn't see any issues, that we both would be able to go home around noon. We need to schedule a visit with his regular pediatrician in about a week or so."

"That's so good to hear. Do you mind if I come along on that visit?"

"No, I don't mind at all. In fact, thank you." "Thank me for what?"

"For being you and wanting to be a part of Tre's life. I must admit, I was scared to even call you about this; I didn't know how you would take it. We hadn't talked in so long, and the last time I saw you it was awkward—not to mention you are with Marla. We haven't even discussed that yet. Troy, I don't know about this. You have a whole girlfriend out there, and you're talking about how you want to be with us and in our lives…you should just go. I will call Precious back and have her take us home."

"Wait, Jasmine, hold on."

"No Troy, there is nothing to wait for. Tre is in the nursery if you want to see him; I need some time to think. Please just go, I need some time."

"Jasmine, hold on—let's talk, please."

"No Troy, I need some time—please leave. We can set something up later. Right now, I need to focus on Tre."

"Ok Jasmine, I don't want to get you all upset."

Jasmine turns her back to Troy and begins sobbing. Troy goes to try to and console her from behind, but Jasmine side steps him. "Please just go; I can't do this right now."

Troy, bewildered by what just happened, stands there for a second pondering how the atmosphere just changed in the blink of an eye without any warning signs. As he walks out, he tries to get his words together, along with fighting back a tear. "Will you at least call me when you get home, so I know everything is ok?"

Jasmine doesn't reply as Troy slowly walks out of the room. Jasmine balls up on the floor crying, her t-shirt soaked with her tears. Clea walks in and sees Jasmine on the ground crying.

"Jasmine, what's wrong? What's wrong? Come on, let's get you up off this floor. Here, sit down right here. What's going on? Is Tre, ok?"

Jasmine, struggling to get her words together, simply nods her head. Clea, being a nurse, tries to calm her breathing to get her to relax. When she finally does, she asks: "Are you ok?"

"Yes, I'm good now. I'm not sure what just happened. Everything was going well—the doctor told me that Tre and I were doing fine and that we will get discharged today, and that Tre wouldn't need a blood transfusion. Then we found out that Troy is Tre's father. Everything was going well— Troy wants to be in both of our lives, and I just lost it and told him to get out. How could I be so stupid? I mean, everything that I ever wanted was right there standing in front of me and I told him to go away."

"You just panicked. You've had a lot going on these last forty-eight hours. Jasmine, your life was almost turned upside down because of this accident. It's understandable; I don't understand how you have been so calm these last two days. I would have been a nervous wreck. Don't be so hard on yourself—everything will work out, just wait and see."

"Hey Mike, can you meet me outside the courthouse?

I really need to talk right now."

"Yea, I can do that. I can be out there in less than a minute."

"Ok cool. I'm parked right out front." "Hey, what's up, Frat?"

"Man, bruh; I don't know—I just don't get it." "Get what, Troy? What's going on?"

"One minute I'm a proud father and on my way to having everything I ever wanted—a family, a woman I love, a son…and the next minute, nothing. She just shuts me out. I don't get it, bruh. Why can't I find real happiness?"

"Whoa, whoa, wait a minute bro, time out! What do you mean? What son? And who are you in love with? Is Marla pregnant?"

"No, bruh—Jasmine's son. Remember, I told you about him? That's my son, bro! Tre is my son. I found out yesterday; that's what I wanted to talk to you and Terrance about."

"How did that happen?"

"Well, I'm sure you heard about the accident between my client and Jasmine, right?"

"Yea, vaguely."

"I went to the hospital to check on my client and Jasmine. Long story short, her son—I mean, our son—was hurt in the accident. He needed blood and he and Jasmine are not a match. She called me and asked if I could get my blood tested because I could be the father and it matched—99.9 percent matched. So, we talked, we kissed, and I thought we were going to work things out, right? I went to the hospital today thinking I can take them home, we can talk some more, and I could spend some time with my son, right? Next thing I know, she is kicking me out of her hospital room and telling me she didn't know about us; talking about how she needs some time. What's up with that? First, she doesn't tell me that it was even a possibility that Tre was mine, then after a great night of apologizing, making up, and thinking about our future, today she kicks me out of her room. I don't get it, bruh—make it make sense. I'm lost! What do I do now?"

"Maybe just give her some time; she has been through a lot these last couple of days. She is just overwhelmed and scared. I know if it was me, I would be going crazy. Think about it—all that's going on right now in her life, and I'm sure she hasn't been sleeping. All this must be taking a toll on her mentally. I know if it were me, they would have me in that rubber room with a straight jacket on; just give her some time and I'm sure she will come around."

"What else can I do? I mean, I understand she has been through a lot, but I just found out about my son. I've already lost so much time not knowing that he was mine. I know that this might sound selfish and all, but I don't want to waste any more time. I know what it's like not to have a father. I lost mine when I was young, and I always told myself that if I ever had children, I wouldn't miss a day with them."

"I hear you, bruh—I do. All I'm saying is let her get home and collect her thoughts; I'm sure she will come around. From what I know about her I don't think she would keep your son away from you."

"Oh, great—just what I needed. Hold one a sec, bruh, this is Marla."

Troy answers the phone. "Hello? Hey Marla, how are you?"

"I'm good—the question is, how are you? I haven't seen or heard from you in a while."

"I know; I've had a lot going on with work and some other things."

"Ok, but are you that busy I can't even get five minutes of your time? The least you could do is give me a phone call. You know, 'hey, Marla; this is Troy. I was just thinking about you' or something; anything is better than ghosting me all together. I thought we were better than that."

"I'm sorry; I could have called; it's just my mind has been all over the place. Not to mention I've been busy with your cousin's murder trial."

"Speaking of that, how is that coming? Will you be able to get her off?"

"We have a good shot at it, it's just going to take some time. We are working on it, though, and we think we have a good plan going forward."

"I heard she was in an accident. How is she doing? I tried calling the hospital, but she had already been discharged."

"She is doing well. I stopped by to see her, and she was ok—just a little shaken, that's all."

"So, when can I see you again? Do I have to schedule some time with your secretary?"

"Oh, you got jokes now, huh?"

"No, I'm serious. What do I need to do to get some time with you?"

"Just be patient with me—I have a lot going on right now, and your cousin's case needs my undivided attention; I'm sure you can understand that."

"Yea, I do! I just want to see you, though. Is that too much to ask?"

"No, it's not. I have court on another matter in a few minutes; I'll be in touch."

"Ok, well…I'll talk to you later. Have a good day." "You do the same."

"Man, Mike, that's another thing—Marla, the woman I was just on the phone with, used to be best friends with Jasmine in college. They had a falling out over some guy and now they can't stand one another. One day we were out to lunch and Jasmine saw us together—you could have cut the tension with a knife; it was so thick. Then today, Jasmine brought her up when we were talking. Me and Marla are not in a serious dating relationship; in fact, we are not in a relationship at all. We have gone out a couple of times and had dinner a few times—that's it; that's all. Nothing more, nothing less. At the end of the day, my heart belongs to Jasmine. I'm all the way in—always have been and always will be."

"Yea, bruh; that much is clear…but do they know that? That's what you need to be telling both. That way, there is no room for any confusion for anyone—both women know exactly where they stand. Being transparent is the best thing you can do for everyone's sake, and in the end both will be better off."

"Yea, your right, bruh! Thank you for the advice; I really appreciate you taking the time to let me vent."

"No problem, bruh; anytime. So, what are you going to do?"

"I'm not exactly sure. I know I need to have a talk with them both at some point. I need to tell Marla that I'm still in love with Jasmine and that we can't be together."

"That's for the best of everyone, and the sooner you tell her, the better."

"Aw man, I can't do that just yet!" "What? Why not?"

"If I tell Marla right now that Jasmine and I are getting back together and that we have a son in common, all hell is going to break out—she would tell everyone just to get back at Jasmine, then her job would fire her. I'm sure she would try to get me disbarred at the very least—this could go very wrong quickly; I must be careful in how this is handled."

"Oh wow…yea, you need to be careful in how you deal with this; things could get ugly for both of you. Well, before you say anything to anybody, you should try to talk to Jasmine and see what she thinks. I'm sure between the two of you that you will find a way to get through all of this. I know this is obvious, but I'm going to tell you anyway—pray about it and ask for guidance."

"I already know, bruh."

"Hit me up if you need to talk or vent, bruh. I'm here for you."

"I know, bruh; and thanks again." "Hey, sis you ready to go?"

"Yes, we are all set. Thank you for coming back."

"No problem, sis. What happened to Troy, though? I thought you all were getting back together, and he was going to bring you guys home?"

"I did, too, and then I realized I have a lot to lose by getting back with Troy—my job, my reputation, my insurance, and so forth. I have worked hard to build my career to not just throw it all away. Not to mention Troy is dating Marla—you know how I feel about that Hoffa! I don't have time for drama with her all over again. I knew she would come after me and Troy—at this point, it's better to leave things well enough alone. Tre must be my priority."

"I get it, sis. But let me ask you this: Do you love him? Simple question."

"Yes, of course I love him, and I always will. The timing is just not right, that's all."

"Sis, sometimes the timing will never be right—just go for it and let God do the rest. His timing is always right when we are in his will. You do what is best for you; I'm ready whenever you are."

"Ok. I got everything."

"When do you go back to the office?"

"I don't know; I guess I should at least go check in and check my email—I know I got thousands of them to go through. Alvin is happy and upset—happy that I'm not there and upset cause I'm not there doing all the work that he wants to take credit for."

"You could call him and let him know that you are just checking in to see if there are any updates on the case, and that you are available by email, phone and Zoom if needed. You will be checking your email periodically."

"You know what? That sounds good, sis. Thank you."

"Hello Alvin, this is Jasmine. I wanted to check in and see if there were any new developments in the case?"

"Well, well, well—so are you back?"

"I never left, Alvin; I was in a car accident if you haven't heard, and my son was severely injured."

"I'm sorry to hear about your son. You don't have to worry about the case; I got this. Focus on being a mommy and take care of your son. I got to run, so I'll talk to you later."

"Um, excuse me…did he just hang up on me? I know he didn't," she says, as the dial tone gets louder and louder in her ear. "This man done lost his mind—he must have forgotten that I run this criminal division! I guess I'm going to have to deal with him when I get back to the office."

"Calm down, sis; he's not worth getting your blood pressure up—and besides, Tre is asleep. Yelling at Alvin is only going to wake up Tre."

"You're right, sis, and thank you for everything. I don't know what I would do without you; you have been my rock, and I appreciate you and everything you have done for us. You're the best little sister anyone could ask for."

"No thanks needed, sis. If Momma didn't teach us anything else, she taught us how to have each other's back."

STRATEGIES

It's been three weeks since Troy has been able to see Jasmine or Tre, and he is feeling some type of way by not being able to see either of them—the only contact he has had has been by scheduled video chats. Just as he is contemplating what to do next, Jasmine is calling via Video Chat.

"Hello? Hey Jasmine; hey friend—how are you?" "We're good. Tre was missing his daddy."

"Oh, yea, I miss you both, too. I was just thinking about the two of you; these last three weeks have been tough not seeing you both. I mean, video calls are cool, but I miss seeing you both in person. I want to be able to hold my son and play with him; I want to cook for you and sit down across the table and have a conversation with you—and before you say it, I already know what you're going to say, but I can't help how I feel. Jasmine, I love you and there is nothing I want more than to be with you. I want us to be a family."

"Troy, I get it, I really do—but understand that this is hard for me, too. You know I love you and want to be with you, but we have some other issues that must be dealt with. Not to mention we are about to start this trial, and there is so much pressure on us to get a conviction in this case. Alvin is absolutely losing his mind and obsessing over this case and every move I make. It feels like he is watching me twenty-four seven. Not to mention you are still with Marla, right?"

"No, we have never been exclusive, and I told her when we met that I wasn't ready for a relationship; I was still trying to get over losing the love of my life. Since we talked at the hospital, I haven't seen her either. Like you, I have been focusing on the case and getting prepared for what's to come. I just pray that we can move past all of this and look to our future. On another note: How has Tre been doing?"

"He's been good. His follow up exam was good, too."

"That's good to hear. Is there any way that you could find some time for me to see him at least?"

"I want you to see him, I really do. I don't want you to ever think that I'm keeping him away from you. It's just this trial and all the press that constantly follows us everywhere we go. How do you suppose we get past that?"

"I was thinking Precious could come over to your house with a doll that's about the same size as Tre, but it's all bundled up. Then, you both leave the house with a bundled child. You leave the house with the doll and Precious leaves with Tre. Then, I would either take an uber or drive my secretary's car and meet them somewhere else, like a restaurant with a play area. I know it's not what either one of us would want, but at least I would be able to spend some time with my son."

"That might work. Let me talk it over with her and see what she thinks."

"Thank you, Jasmine; I really appreciate you being willing to do this."

"You don't have to thank me, Troy—you're his father and I want him to have a relationship with you."

"Wow! You know, I never thought I would hear those words—I like the way it sounds. I'm a father and even better: I'm Tre's father. I'm a dad!" Troy exclaims with tremendous pride.

"You're funny, but it does my heart good that you feel this way. I will talk to you later."

"Love you, son. Love you, Jasmine."

"We love you, too, Troy." The video call ends. "Well, little man—it's time for Momma to go to work and for you to go to day care with TT Precious."

"Jasmine, when you are settled in your office today, can you please step into my office? I need to talk to you," Matt asks.

"Sure Matt, I'll be right there."

"Let me first start by saying I know you have a lot on your plate, with getting over your accident, your son, and this murder case. However, because we are so thin right now, I need you to handle this other murder case, as well—and before you say it, I know we are getting close to the senator's trial date. However, I need you to handle this simple case for me. A young homeless woman stabbed her boyfriend after an argument. We have her confession on video and the murder weapon but there are no eyewitnesses—nothing. Desi was going to handle it, but she is out sick, and we are at the end of their speedy trial demand. This trial shouldn't last more than a day or two, at the most. I'll have the file brought into your office."

"Well, it sounds like I have no other choice in the matter. I'll get started right way with getting caught up to speed."

Jasmine begins going over the case files and starts seeing minor discrepancies in the police report versus the confession. She picks up the phone and calls Matt. "We have a problem with this case. When the police first arrived and talked with the defendant, she told them that he had beat her up earlier in the day, and when he got back home after going out drinking and getting high with his friends, she was in the kitchen cleaning, when he came into the kitchen and started to beat her up again. He struck her in the face and then begin to choke her at the counter, which is where the knife was that she used to kill him with.

"In the recorded confession, the defendant didn't mention anything about the previous fight or him going out drinking with his friends and then coming back to beat her—it only states that they got into an argument, and then she stabbed him because she couldn't take arguing with him anymore. Also, in the police report, it doesn't say anything about the black eye, the bruises, and the broken ribs she sustained. I did some digging after reading her statement and found out that she had previously called the police for domestic violence—and on several occasions, the officers never did anything or took any kind of action. They only told her to file an order of protection. In the past six months, she has filed three orders of protection, and in each of the three orders of protection, she claims that he violated them and continued to come over and beat her whenever he wanted to while telling her that he would kill her and her family if she showed up to court—which is why she never showed up to court to get the orders of protection extended. I took a deeper look into his background, and back in the late nineties he was convicted of assault with a deadly weapon, aggravated discharge, and attempted murder of his girlfriend. He also had a significant tie to the local gang and its members. Matt, I think we should not be pursuing this case, or at least file a motion to continue the trial to give us more time to figure out what exactly happened on the night in question. Matt, this was self-defense. I don't know how they could have missed all of this, but I don't feel comfortable prosecuting this woman based solely off the confession—not to mention this so-called confession came thirty-six hours later and with her not getting any sleep; I can't in good conscious go after her for this. I don't know how Desi missed these things, but this woman is innocent."

"Jasmine, we have a signed video confession and the murder weapon. We know they had an argument and she stabbed him—that's all we need to know. This case is moving forward. You will prosecute her, and you will send her to jail for an exceedingly long time."

"I can't do that! I'm sorry, Matt—I've never told you that I can't, but I will not prosecute this case. I've seen too many poor minorities go to jail for this type of stuff and I will not be a part of this system any longer. I need some time away to think."

"Jasmine, I need you on this case and for you to second chair the senator's case."

"No, you don't—you got Alvin. Let him do it. I need some time away; I need at least a couple of weeks."

"I'm sorry, Jasmine, but we can't afford to give you that type of time off, especially right now with us being shorthanded. Either you do this and the other trial, or I'm afraid we will have to let you go."

"Well, you do what you feel you must do, Matt, and I'll do the same. You have a blessed day. I will see you around."

"Wait, Jasmine! Can we at least talk about this?"

"No, Matt—my mind is made up; this is it for me. I can no longer do this with a clear conscious knowing that we are prosecuting innocent people even when we know the truth. I'll send someone for my things."

Jasmine hangs up the phone and walks out of the office. Alvin is standing next to the fax machine with a smirk on his face, as if he had overheard her conversation with Matt. She ignores him and proceeds to walk out the door. Once she gets to her car, she takes a deep breath, and a single tear slowly runs down her face. An indescribable peace comes over her as she takes off to pick up Tre.

"Hey Precious, I'm on my way to pick up Tre. I just quit my job!"

"Jasmine, stop playing—you did not just quit that job that you love."

"For real, I really did just quit. I told my boss I couldn't take it anymore and I needed to take a break for awhile. He didn't want to give it to me, so I told him that I was leaving. I grabbed my coat and purse and walked out, and you know what? I feel great about it. It's weird, because I never thought I would leave there and if I did, I would feel some type of way—but I don't. I feel free, like a load has been lifted off my shoulders; like I have been holding my breath for years and now I can finally let it out and just breathe."

"Well, if you're ok, I'm ok."

"Do you have any kids at the house other than Tre?" "I do, but they are about to leave so I'll be done for the day by the time you get here."

"Ok great, I'm going to stop at the store and pick up a bottle of wine and we are going to celebrate a new beginning!"

"Sounds good to me—I'm here for it all."

"Shay, Shay! Come here, quick! Shay, come here; you have some mail!"

"Is that what I think it is, Momma!"

"Yes, baby—it's a letter from Georgetown." "Momma, I can't believe it. I'm so nervous, my hands are shaking. What if they declined my application, Momma?"

"If they did that, then they didn't deserve you anyways."

"Can we pray before we open it, Momma?"

"Yes baby. Father, I thank you for always listening to us. We come to you as humbly as we know how. Father, you already know what Shay desires and for what she has worked so hard for. If it is your will, please let this be an admittance letter, and if it's not what you would like for her, to give her the peace of mind to be able to accept it. Father, I pray that either way, you guide her footsteps and put the right people in her path that she can learn and grow from. We ask all these things in you sons Jesus' name, Amen."

Shay anxiously waiting with bated breath. "You open it, Momma; I can't." Tears begin to flow as her hands begin to shake. She grabs Shay and hugs her tight.

"Thank you, Lord!" She screams out: "Shay, you got in baby! You have been accepted to the University of Georgetown!" Shay falls to the floor, screaming and crying—goose bumps fill her body. She couldn't believe it! "Let's go!" she yells.

"I told you, baby, that you would get in. You have done the work, kept your grades up, and all the service work you did—they couldn't help but to let you in, baby."

"Oh my God, Momma! I can't believe it."

"Believe it, baby. This fall you will be attending the University of Georgetown. I'm so proud of you! This is just the start for you and all the remarkable things you are going to accomplish in life."

"Thank you, Momma; I owe it all to you. You have shown me so much and have poured into me. You're the best role model, best friend, and most of all the best mother anyone could ever ask for."

"Aw, thank you, baby girl. You are the best daughter I could have ever asked for. Blessings are coming our way, Shay."

"You're right, Momma—and you're next. I know you're going to be proven innocent when your trial is done."

"That's right, and then we can put this whole thing behind us. I've also been meaning to talk to you about that night. Have you been having trouble sleeping lately? I've noticed you have been up walking late at night, and a couple of times you have cried out in your sleep—by the time I got to your door, you were back asleep, so I didn't want to wake you."

"I have had a couple of nightmares about you being in jail and about that night."

"Why didn't you come to me and talk to me, baby?"

"I don't know, Momma. I didn't want to bother you, I guess."

"Baby girl, you're never a bother to me and I am always here for you. I've had a couple of nightmares myself lately, and I have been meaning to talk to you about us going to counseling. I'm thinking it will give us both the release we need. I wish I had done it years ago instead of waiting for so long to properly deal with this issue."

"If you think it would help, then I'm all for it."

"Ok, great. I'll get something set up after the trial is over. In the meantime, if you ever feel like you want to talk, you know you can always come to me, and we can deal with it together."

"I know, Momma. I love you."

"I love you, too, Shay. Now, let me get into this kitchen and cook you a celebratory meal. Oh, I'm so proud of you, Shay!"

"Thank you!"

Troy and Terrance are now back in the office going over their strategy plans.

"Terrance, is there anything else that you can think of that we need to do, or questions that we need to ask?"

"No, I think we have covered it all. We have a solid game plan; the strategy makes sense and not only is it believable, it's the truth. If we get the jury that we are looking for, then I think we will get a not guilty verdict. It would be hard pressed to convict her once they know that the senator wasn't what he said he was, and how he has been sexually assaulting women for years and, because of his status, getting away with it. It's really a classic case of how men of power have taken advantage of their place in life to assault women. After this trial is over, let's try to think of a way that we can help battered women or people who are in domestic violence situations. Those statistics you told me about are still blowing my mind—and what's worse is that a lot of it goes unreported. I would also like to start donating something to mental illness; maybe start doing some fundraisers for those two causes."

"Those are some great ideas, Troy. I've been thinking about this as well and was meaning to bring it up to you. I'm glad to see that we are on the same page with this—it must be a sign that we need to make this happen."

"I agree. On another note, what's going on with you, Jasmine, and the baby?"

"I finally got to spend some time with my son yesterday, and bro—it was amazing. I never knew I could fall in love with someone so fast and so deep. Tre is an amazing kid! He is smart, full of personality and energy— that boy didn't sit down for the whole visit. Then, at the end he gave me the biggest hug and squeezed me so tight; it was as if he had known me for years and that just melted my heart. I just wish my momma were here to meet him—she would spoil him rotten."

"Yea, she would have. I have a feeling he will still be spoiled, and I can't wait to meet him."

"He is going to love his Uncle Terrance." "What about Jasmine?"

"That's even more complicated. I'm not exactly sure where we stand. What's crazy is that we both know that we love each other, but we have so much standing between the us—her job being the main one, and then there is the Marla situation. I haven't seen her that much, and I told her that I need to focus on the case at hand. She doesn't like it, but she says she understands. Deep down, she knows that something is going on with me and that I have been avoiding her. It's all driving me crazy, T. On one hand, I have the woman I love, who is the mother of my son—she is smart, intelligent, someone who I know understands me, and we share the same taste in music and art. She loves God. What more could a man ask for, right? Then you have Marla—she is very wealthy, intelligent, and we also share similar taste in music and art—not sure if she has a relationship with God or not because she has never talked about it. She also seems needy and clingy, and it's that part that pushes me away. At the end of the day, my heart is with Jasmine. I just wish that there were some way, somehow, that we could be together."

"Troy, it sounds like you know what you need to do and who you want to be with. If that's the case, then go after what you want."

"It's not that easy, T."

"I know it's not that easy, but out of all the years I've known you, I have never seen you back down or not obtain something you went after. So, if Jasmine and your family is what you want, then go for it and don't stop. Pray about it and I'm sure you will find your way."

"Thanks T, I appreciate it. What's up with you and Lisa? I haven't heard you talk about her in a while."

"I guess you can say we are taking it slow, trying to figure things out as we go."

"Nothing wrong with that—slow can be good if that is what you want."

"Crazy thing is, I don't know what I want. One minute I want to be married and do the family thing and then that fades, and I enjoy being single and doing my own thing and having my own space. Is that wrong?"

"No, I can't say that it's wrong if that's how you feel. I'm glad you're taking the time to find out, though. You should take your own advice and pray for your situation, as well."

"I will if you will, brother."

"Man, will you look at us? If this were ten years ago, we would have never been having this conversation," Troy laughs. "Me a father, and you thinking about settling down! Whoa."

"Yea, that's funny, Troy. Oh, how times have changed!"

"They have, and I guess so have we. I think it's time me and Jasmine had a face-to-face conversation—I need to tell her how I feel so we can come to some type of plan to be together or go our separate ways and learn how to co-parent Tre."

"That is a great idea."

"Hey Jasmine, I hope I didn't catch you at an inconvenient time. Are you still at the office?"

"It's fine, and no, I'm not in the office—what's up?"

"I know you said you needed some time to think, and I have tried to respect that—I think I have respected that wish. I was hoping that we could meet just for a few minutes; I would like to talk about our future with each other and with Tre."

"Ok, that is fine. Where would you like to meet? Do you have any place in mind? If not, we can meet at our spot in the park."

"The park would be perfect."

"What time would you like to meet?"

"I have a few more things to take care of here at the office, so maybe around seven if that would work for you?"

"Yes, that would be fine. I have a few things that I need to talk to you about, as well, so your timing is perfect."

"Sounds good; I will talk to you soon, then.

Goodbye."

"Judging by that big grin on your face now, she agreed to meet and talk with you?" Terrance asks.

"Yea, she did T—we are meeting tonight at seven at the park, and there was something different in her voice this time. She seemed more receptive to meeting and talking about our future. I pray that she does not change her mind again."

"Well, there is only one way to find out—we will see what happens later tonight."

"Yes, we will see. Let's get back to work, though. Do you think Ms. Henderson is prepared enough to testify?"

"I believe so—we grilled her hard, and she withstood it and stayed levelheaded. Are we going to let her testify?"

"I still don't know yet; that depends on what the state presents to the jury. The one thing that worries me, though, is if we would have to put Shay on the stand. I'm not sure if Ms. Henderson will let us do that or if she can take seeing her daughter grilled on the stand."

"Oh my God, Terrance. I don't know how we could have missed this, and it just hit me. Now, the senator assaulted Ms. Henderson, his wife, and Shay, right? If that's the case, it makes sense that if he did it to those three, there may be more he has done it too, as well. If we can establish a pattern of behavior, then we may not have to use Shay at all, and it will be easier to prove our self-defense claim."

"That sounds great and all Troy, but we only have a couple of days to get that together. It's not like we can put an ad in the paper. How do we go about finding these women and how do we get them to testify? Most women like Patricia want to forget about it and never talk about it."

"I don't know T, but we must try—and this gives us an even better shot at getting this case dismissed. Call the private investigator again and have him see what he can dig up—have him start with past female employees or volunteers that has worked with the senator or for him. Did any of them quit or leave suddenly for no reason? What was the mood around the campaign or office?"

"Ok, I'm on it, Troy; I will go take care of this while you get ready for tonight. Go, get your family, bro, and don't try to prepare for it like you're doing your closing statements. Go speak from your heart and let it flow; show her your heart and things will work out. I promise!"

"Thanks bro, I will talk to you later and let me know if he hears anything."

"I will, and you let me know how your talk with Jasmine goes, as well."

"Hey, sis, it's me. I just got a call from Troy, and he wants to meet me at seven o'clock tonight. Can you do me a huge favor and watch Tre a little longer? I want to go home and get ready to meet Troy, and then I'll be over to celebrate and pick up Tre."

"Ok, that is fine. Are you going to tell him about your job?"

"Yes, I'm going to tell him—I do not want him to hear it from someone else."

"Now, the bigger question is, what you are going to do if he tells you he wants to get back with you?"

"Honestly, I don't know. All of this is happening so suddenly, and I haven't had enough time to think it through— that's why I want to go home, clean up, and get my thoughts together."

"I can understand that. Whatever you do, I'm behind you."

"Ok, I will talk to you later."

WHAT WAS MEANT TO BE

"Good evening, Jasmine; you look nice. Thank you for meeting with me."

"Thank you, and so do you. If you don't mind, could I go first?"

"Sure, go right ahead."

"Jasmine, ever since we broke up, I have had a lot of time to think about why we broke up and my role in it all. I have come to realize that when you're in a relationship, it's two people working together in every way possible—it's a partnership with equal sides. It's two people giving one-hundred percent of everything they have. I didn't understand that back then, but now I do. I get it. Jasmine, I love you with everything in me, and my life has not been the same since you left. It's like a piece of me has been missing. All my life, I have wanted a family, but I didn't know what it took to keep a family because it was always just me and my mom. That day we were in the hospital; it was like a light bulb turned on and I realized this is what I had been wanting in my life— and what I want for the rest of my life: a woman that I love and a child to take care of and love. It was one of the best feelings I have ever experienced. Even though the circumstances were not ideal, it still meant a lot to me. Since then, I haven't been able to think about anything else. Even if Tre were not my son, I would still want to have you both in my life. Whenever I think about anything good going on, now or in the future, I can always see you by my side. I want to come home to you and tell you about my day, good or bad. I want to celebrate accomplishments and milestones with you. I would love to have you come home and have dinner cooked, with Tre and I are waiting to hear about your day or celebrate your accomplishments and milestones. I know I am rambling, and I apologize—what I'm trying to say is that I am in love with you, and I would love it if you gave us another chance. We can start slowly and move as slowly as you want. Oh, and as far as Marla is concerned, I haven't seen her since before your accident. I had my doubts about being with her because I still had feelings for you, so I had told her that I wasn't ready for a relationship. Ok, I'm done."

"Whew, Troy, that was a lot. I don't think you have ever opened up like that. I can see that there has been some growth. Ever since that day Tre and I ran into you in the park, I have wondered what this moment would look like, how it would feel, what you would say, and what I would say. That day, so many memories came flooding back and if I'm honest with you and myself, I have never stopped loving you. I secretly prayed that you were Tre's father and that we could make it work, and now that moment is here…I would be a fool if I did not take this opportunity, this second chance at the greatest love of my life. This is what I prayed for, and God has answered my prayers. So yes, Troy, I would love to give this another shot. As for Marla, we will have to deal with that very carefully; she is conniving and calculating, to say the least."

"Just so I'm clear…you want to get back together again, right?" Troy asks.

"Yes, Troy, I want us to try again." Troy gives Jasmine the biggest bear hug, lifting her up off the ground as they begin to kiss.

"Aw man, I am so happy. I could scream!" His eyes begin to water. "I love you so much Jasmine, and I promise I will do better and be a better boyfriend."

"I know Troy, and I will be a better girlfriend and communicator myself; I will not just assume you know what I'm thinking."

"Oh, what about your job and Alvin…how do you want to play this?"

"That, we will not have to worry about any longer," Jasmine says with a grin.

"What's that about? Why the grin?"

"Well, I quit my job today, effective immediately." "Are you serious about that? You loved your job." "I did, but they wanted me to prosecute this woman

for a murder that was clearly self-defense to me, and no one cared. I'm tired of going after poor minorities who have done nothing wrong, and yet I'm supposed to be the one who takes their freedom. I can't be a part of that any longer, so I quit, and it felt so good. I was so relieved."

"Wow, I'm shocked. What are you going to do now?"

"I don't know, but I want to do something meaningful; something that will have an impact and an impression in my community and for my community."

"Well, whatever I can do to help or assist you, know that I have you. If you need some office space until you get some things figured out, you can come to our office. Oh, Jasmine—you don't know how happy you have made me."

"Well, that makes two of us. Let us go pick up our baby, grab a bite, and then go to my place."

"Now that sounds like a great idea!" Jasmine and Troy embrace again while sharing a kiss and head back to their cars holding hands.

"Hey, Precious, I'm here. Can you open the door?"

"Ok, here I come. What's going on? I thought you would be gone longer?" Precious asks.

"Well, it doesn't take that long when you're in love." Jasmine steps to the side and Troy is standing right behind her.

"Hey Precious, it's good to see you again," he says. "It's good to see you, too. Now, what is going on you two? Somebody tell me what just happened."

"Well, after some soul searching and open communication, Troy and I have decided to work on being together again and since I quit my job, we don't have to worry about that anymore, either. We are going to be a family." Jasmine leaves Troy and Precious standing in the living room and then returns from a back room with Tre in her arms. "Tre, look: your daddy is here!"

"Oh, come here son! How is my big boy, huh? How are you doing, son?" Troy hugs and squeezes Tre, then kisses him on the cheek and forehead. "Hey Tre, it's me, it's your Daddy!"

"Well, we really have something to celebrate now," Precious says.

"Yes, we do!"

"I'm so proud of you both. You all make a great couple and will be great parents! I pray you both remember to keep him first in everything you do."

"I'm sure we will," says Troy as he continues to hug Tre. Jasmine and Precious marvel at how loving Troy is with his son. Precious whispers, "You got a good one there, sis!"

"I know, girl. And this time we will make it work." "Did you tell him you quit your job?"

"Yes, I did tell him and he's ok with it. In fact, he offered me space in his office if I needed it. I don't know what I'm going to do just yet, but at least I have an option now."

"That's true. I have faith that God will lead me where he wants me to go. I'm in no hurry, so that's a plus in my favor, as well. Troy, are you ready to go? It's time for Tre to get ready for bed. You can come help and read him a story before bed if you would like."

"I would love that! What do you think Tre? Would you like Daddy to come read to you?" Tre smiles as if he understood the question. "Let's get you ready then, big man." They get Tre ready and say their goodbyes.

Jasmine and Troy pull up to Jasmine's house; Troy gets out and goes to get Tre out of the backseat of the car. Jasmine is not accustomed to having someone help her with Tre, so she grins and grabs Tre's things from the back of the car. Once inside, Jasmine begins getting Tre ready for bed as Troy sits in the rocking chair next to Tre's bed, looking through the books to see which one he would read to Tre. He chooses JoJo's Learning Adventures. "This looks good, and it's written by one of my favorite authors, Royce Dixon Sr."

"That's an excellent choice. He loves that one and the illustrations," Jasmine says. Before Troy could get to the end, Tre is fast asleep with Jasmine and Troy standing there, looking over him.

"Look at our son, Jasmine, can you believe it? I wish my mother could have seen this. Her first grandson—she would have loved this. He is so perfect."

"Yes, he is, and so are you, Mr. Brooks. Thank you for being who you are. I really appreciate it. You could have easily hated me and walked away, and you didn't. You're here loving our son and for that, I am forever grateful!"

"No need to thank me. I'm just giving back what God has given me. When my mom passed, it was one of the hardest things I have ever had to deal with, and you stood by my side; even when I was being a jerk, you still stayed and offered help. I was a fool for not seeing what a beautiful thing I had right in front of me. I'm so glad that God saw fit to give us another chance to get it right—and this time I will get it right, that I can promise you!" Troy reaches out his hand and pulls Jasmine closer to him as they stare into each other's eyes. "I love you, Jasmine!"

"I love you, too, Troy. Follow me, sir." Jasmine takes the lead, taking him into the bedroom, and closes the door behind her. "Have a seat right there." She slowly moves to the front of Troy and stands in between his open legs. She begins to remove his tie, kissing him seductively while doing so. Next, she starts to unbutton his shirt. The room begins to heat up and so does Troy. The excitement begins to build while she slowly takes his shirt off, subtly kissing his neck, and then starts a sultry strip tease with a silk scarf that she had tied around her neck and slowly dances in front of Troy. Troy is mesmerized with Jasmine's moves and how her naked body was starting to appear as she slowly unzipped her cat suit. As the anticipation builds, so does the bulge of his manhood. Jasmine, fully undressed, pushes Troy back on the bed carefully and gently, to not damage his swollen package, and begins to undress his lower half one pant leg at a time until he is naked, as well. Jasmine is now fully in control and Troy is now at her mercy. No one could ever love him the way Jasmine is doing right now—every one of his senses is on high alert, from his sense of touch, sight, smell, hearing, and taste; all five senses are now working together with everything that Jasmine does. Troy rolls Jasmine over and now returns the favor to her. His strong, powerful hands grip her breast. She feels up and down his chiseled arms, like an African warrior or a Greek God. Troy is an experienced and gifted talent with his tongue, and he is giving Jasmine all she could handle or want.

"Come here, Daddy; I want to feel you inside of me." Troy was extremely happy to oblige in her request. He slides even with her, while staring into her eyes, as if he could see her very essence. She takes him not only into her, but her very soul, to where no man has ever been able to connect with her. Every move is as if they had rehearsed this choreographed dance; they are so in sync with one another that every desire was met, every need was fulfilled until they both had their fill. Both now spent on every level lay there, and for a time, the earth stood still; all they could do was lay there holding one another. After some time had passed, Jasmine asked Troy if he could spend the night—after what had just happened, how could he say no?

"Of course, I can. And in the morning, I could make you breakfast if you want."

"No Troy, not this time. I'll make you breakfast while you play with your son and get to know him more."

The following morning, as promised, Jasmine is up cooking breakfast while Troy and Tre are in the living room playing on the floor. "Wow, Jasmine! Breakfast smells good in there. Do you need any help?"

"No, I got this, and I'm almost done." A few minutes later, Jasmine walks into the living room and just stares for a second at Tre and Troy on the floor, playing and having a fun time. She realizes that this is all she has ever wanted for herself and their son—a loving man and a loving father! "Troy, you can eat now."

"Ok, we are on our way." When Troy gets into the kitchen, his plate has been made and sitting on the table. It's all his favorite breakfast foods: bacon, sausage gravy, pancakes, scrambled eggs with cheese, and orange juice. "Wow Jasmine, you outdid yourself with all of this." As they all prepare to eat, Troy, being the neat freak, notices that the kitchen is clean, and everything is back in its place. He doesn't say anything, but he can tell that something has drastically changed since the last time they were together— that doesn't even matter now. All that matters is that they are back together again.

"Jasmine, do you mind if I ask you why you left the state attorney's office?"

"No, not at all. So yesterday, I got to the office and Matt called me in to his office. He proceeds to ask me to cover this murder trial because Desi is out. He says it's an open and shut case, right? We have the murder weapon and a videotaped confession—a slam dunk. The thing is, that he wanted me to go to trial in like two days, right before our big murder case with the senator and Ms. Henderson. I start looking through the file and there are a lot of discrepancies, and I didn't feel comfortable trying to get this woman convicted on a crime she didn't commit—especially since it was self-defense. The more I investigated the file, the more I realized he didn't care about justice or poor people being treated fairly. This woman was beaten on several occasions—even that night, he had beat her before going out with his friend. He then returns home drunk and starts to beat her up again, but this time she fought back. Her confession was different than the report that was taken on scene, and it had no mention of her black eye or broken ribs, not to mention the previous orders of protection she had filed against him. All I had asked for was a little time to see what really happened that day. Matt seemed adamant about prosecuting her and I couldn't do it; I couldn't see sending another person to prison for the rest of their lives. So, I quit. Troy, I want to have influence in the world. I want to feel like what I do matters and that at the end of the day, I can go home and feel good about myself and the job I've done."

"Wow! I would have never thought you felt that way; I thought you were looking forward to being the next state's attorney."

"I was, but in the back of my mind, I always wanted something more meaningful. Don't get me wrong—I did love it for a period, but as time went on, things began to change, and it was all about the conviction rate and not justice. This last case that he wanted me to do just proved it."

"Sounds to me like you might want to start your own defense attorney practice and hand pick your cases."

"The thought crossed my mind. I'll think it over."

"Ok, sounds good. I'm sure that whatever you decide will be what's best."

"Is that your phone ringing?"

"Yea, I think so. Do you remember where I put it?" "I think it's over there on the end table."

"Hey T, I missed your call; what's up?"

"I've got some good news and some sad news. The good news is that we think we found two women who may have been assaulted. The sad news is that one doesn't want to come out to the public and the other one no one has seen since she stopped working for him."

"Ok well…keep looking and see if we can meet with the other one. We need to get her to testify."

"Ok, I'm on it. How did your talk go with Jasmine?"

"I'm here now with her and I will call you back later."

"Alright, I'll talk to you later."

"Hey, Jasmine, I need to get to the office. Can I come back and see you and Tre later?"

"Of course, you can."

"Ok, I'll call you later then. Love you." "I love you, too, Troy!"

"Bye little man! Daddy will see you later, too!"

"Hey, Terrance, I'm leaving Jasmine's now. Where are you?"

"I'm at the office now."

"Ok, good. What's your day looking like?" "I'm done for the day; what's going on?"

"I want to work on the strategy some more before we head into this trial on Monday. We have three days to find this woman or get the other one to talk. I'm pulling into our parking lot now; let's meet in the conference room."

"Ok, that's fine. I'm heading there now."

"What all do we know about these two women right now?"

"One quit right around the same time four and five years ago. The first one—Kimberly Russell, who quit five years ago—was working as an aide to Senator Johnson; she was a college graduate student at Georgetown studying political science, and this was a part of her internship. She is a single mom with a five-year-old daughter, with no other family that we could find and is now working for a network as a political analyst. We are working to get her phone number, so we can at least try to convince her to tell us why she quit, or anything she may know about Senator Johnson.

"The other woman, Ms. Jocelyn Aberra, quit four years ago. She was also a student at Georgetown doing her internship with the senator; she was a law student there. After she quit, she didn't go back to school, and no one has seen or heard from her since. We googled her name and found a woman with that name who committed suicide a couple of years ago. We are trying to get a copy of her death certificate to see if the same person as the one who worked for Senator Johnson."

"Ok, so both went to the same school. Didn't Senator Johnson go there, too?"

"I believe so. Hold on, let me look it up. Yea, according to his bio, he did go there—he finished with his law degree and he minored in political science. That could be the connection—he's targeting young students, with little to no family to come intern for him, and then he assaults them, knowing the probability of them saying anything to anyone would be slim because of who he is and how well connected he is; he uses that power to control them and the situation. Now that we have established a pattern, let's walk through this whole night. It still feels like we are missing something."

"First, we have Senator Johnson, a young up and coming council member who was being mentored by Mr. Bordeaux. Senator Johnson then rapes Patricia Henderson when she was a teenager. She keeps quiet so that she doesn't embarrass her father and family. Years later, she meets a young woman named Michelle Leaper in a shelter for battered women. She has been beaten up by her then boyfriend, Senator Craig Johnson. Ms. Henderson then befriends this battered woman, who then leaves the shelter based on promises by Mr. Johnson, unbeknown to Ms. Henderson. Years later at a fundraising event, they ran into one another again. This time, Ms. Leaper is now known as Mrs. Johnson, the senator's new wife. Ms. Henderson, putting two and two together, knows that Senator Johnson was the one that beat her. Now, on the night of the murder: Shay comes in to get some papers signed by the senator; he's intoxicated and starts to assault Shay, and her mother—who just happens to be looking for her daughter—walks into the room and sees her daughter being attacked with her panties on the floor. Patricia then attacks the senator and is overpowered, finding herself being pinned down. As this is going down, Michelle, the senator's wife, comes in looking for her husband, sees him on top of her friend, then goes into a rage and attacks the senator with a letter opener. Patricia tries to render aid to help the senator, but it's too late for him—which explains the blood on her clothes and her hands. She also tells her daughter to go home, burn her clothes, and to not talk to anyone. She then gets the car for Mrs. Johnson, drives to the side of the building, so as not to be seen. Mrs. Johnson gets in the car; they drive to the hotel and get a room. She takes the key to Mrs. Johnson, gets her settled into the room, and then heads back to the party afterward, where she is apprehended by the police. I think that about covers it."

"Yes, I think you're right, Troy. I can see those wheels turning. What's up?"

"I'm just looking at all the lives this man has ruined over the years. In the case of Patricia and Shay, that's two generations of women that will have to deal with the fallout from his selfish acts."

"Yea, that's terrible. In Patricia's case, she has been carrying around her hidden feelings for years. What a strong, remarkable woman—and to think she has been helping other women deal with this, as well, taking on all their hurt and pain."

"I know, right?! We need more people like her. We must get her acquitted."

"Agreed. Can you call Mike back and see if he has heard anything else?"

"Hello Mike, do you have anything for me yet?"

"I did find out that Ms. Aberra is indeed deceased. She committed suicide shortly after she stopped working with the senator. I am emailing you a copy of her death certificate now. I don't have a phone number yet for Ms. Russell."

"Ok. Thanks."

"Check your email; he sent over the death certificate." Troy pulls out his cell phone to check his email.

"Oh man, Terrance, you are not going to believe this— Ms. Joycelyn Aberra's mother is Marla Bordeaux."

"You can't be serious."

"I'm so serious. The address listed here is the same address as the Bordeaux estate; it also has Marla's name as the mother."

"Now, how does she fit into this?"

"Well, Senator Johnson does know the family well; we know that much from what Patricia and Marla has told us. They were always having fundraisers, so that could be how they met—not to mention the Georgetown connection. Do you think that she committed suicide because she had been abused by the senator, too?"

"I mean, it's possible. Are you going to ask Marla?" "We should ask Patricia first."

"Yea, I agree. Let me call her now and see if she can come in to talk to us."

"Hello, Ms. Henderson; this is Troy Brooks. Do you think you could come into the office today? We are working on your case, and we think that we have something that will help your case."

"Ok, what is it?"

"Well, we would rather talk to you in person."

"Ok, well I'm right around the corner from you now, and I could stop in if it's not going to be too long."

"No, it shouldn't take long at all."

"She said that she would be here shortly."

"Ok, great. It seems like the more we discover, the more we truly don't know, and our time is growing shorter. Monday will be here before you know it."

"Excuse me, Mr. Brooks; Mr. Mays—Ms. Patricia Henderson is here to see you."

"Ok, you can bring her in, thank you. Ms. Henderson, thank you for coming in so quickly. The reason we wanted you to come in is so we could ask you a few more questions and tie up some loose ends."

"Terrance and I have been building a case for your self-defense claim, and we have established that Senator Johnson has been abusing women for years. We know that he assaulted his wife, you, and your daughter—and now we know there are at least two other young women that use to work with him. A Kimberly Russell, who no longer lives there, and then we have a Jocelyn Aberra."

"Jocelyn, what does she have to do with this. She's dead; how can she help?"

"That's kind of what we want to talk to you about.

How did you know Ms. Aberra?"

"She is Marla's adopted daughter." "Was she a student at Georgetown?"

"Yes, she was. She is the reason Shay wants to go there. They were close, and Shay looked up to her."

"Did you know she did an internship working for Senator Johnson?"

"No, I had no idea. When she went off to college, I didn't see her much. She and Shay stayed in contact by video calling one another. What does all this have to do with my case?"

"Well, we don't know for sure; however, we think that the senator may have assaulted her, as well. We know that she did some campaign work with him and shortly after she started, she left abruptly then, not long after that, she committed suicide. Do you know if she left a note or anything that might give us more insight?"

"No, I mean, right before she took her life, there were rumors throughout the family that she might have been pregnant, but no one knew for sure."

"That's interesting. The other women who we think was also assaulted left in the same manner. Not long after she started, she quit and that was five years ago, and she now has a five-year-old daughter. The only thing though is that she won't talk to us about it—not yet anyway; we are going to be reaching out to her again as soon as we can to see if she will talk to us. In the meantime, I think we should talk to Marla and see if she can fill in some of the blanks for us. Do you think she would be willing to talk to us?" Terrance explains.

"I'm not sure. Marla was very hurt and deeply saddened when Jocelyn died. She had to seek therapy to deal with it. I'll give her a call."

"Thank you, Patricia, for coming in and talking to us. This will help us a lot with your case and will help tell the story of how abusive he was. When the jury hears about all of this, they will have no choice but to acquit you. We will keep you abreast of any new developments."

"Thank you, please do."

"Our secretary will see you out. Have a good day." "You two do the same."

"Terrance, I think it would be best if I did this one on my own. She may open up more to me if it's just the two of us," Troy says.

"Yea, you're right."

"While I'm doing that, can you try to contact Ms. Aberra again?"

"Hello Marla, this is Troy. Are you at home?" "Yes, I'm home. What's up?"

"Well, I wanted to stop by and talk to you."

"Oh, now you have time for me and you want to talk."

"I told you I have been busy working on your cousin's case. Remember? The one you hired me to do?"

"Ok, so what do you need?"

"I'd rather see you and talk to you in person, which is why I'm calling. I am headed to your house now, if that's ok."

"Yes, that's fine. I will be here."

Troy pulls up to the Bordeaux estate and stops at the gate to marvel at all its beauty before driving on. Marla greets him at the door wearing a sheer robe with a skimpy bathing suit underneath, her perfume filling the air with its alluring notes. Marla reaches to embrace Troy, but he is hesitant and reluctant. Marla notices but doesn't say anything; she could feel that something was off between them now.

"So, Troy, what is so urgent that we needed to talk?" Marla asks.

"Terrance and I have been attempting to put together a strategy for Patricia's case and we have had a bunch of new developments. One thing that we have learned about Senator Johnson is that he has abused many young women over the years; he has a history of sexual assaulting young vulnerable women. In the past, he has had many young women who worked for him in some capacity or another, mostly interns."

"What does any of that have to do with me? I've never worked for him, nor have I ever been assaulted by him."

"I know that. I'm here to talk to you about your adopted daughter, Joycelyn. Can you tell me about her?"

"Wait what? Do you think he assaulted my daughter, too?"

"I'm not sure, but that's what we are trying to find out. A year before she started working for the senator, there was another young lady who held the same position as your daughter and suddenly quit her position for no apparent reason. My team tracked her down and found out that right after she left, she had a child. We believe that child is Senator Johnson's child and that's the reason she left. A year later, Joycelyn takes the job and then she leaves abruptly with no warning. So, what we are trying to establish is a pattern of sexual assault. I can't get into any more specifics with you yet because our case is ongoing and confidential. Did Jocelyn ever talk to you about what was wrong before she passed?"

"I knew something was wrong when she came home on that last break; she was so withdrawn, which was not like her. She would just sit in her room for hours on end. At first, I thought she was working on some school project or something, and every time I asked her if she was ok, she would say she was fine—but I could see in her face and in her eyes that she wasn't. Then there was this one time we had a fundraising event here at the house and she never came out of her room. I knew then something was wrong, because that was not like her at all. When she stopped having friends come over, I knew something was wrong and finally convinced her to see a psychiatrist. She did that a couple of times a month for about two months before she took her life."

"Marla, I hate to ask you this, but was Joycelyn pregnant?"

Tears begin to flow down her face and her lips begin to quiver. "Yes, she was pregnant. They say she was about three and a half months at the time of her death."

"Did she have a boyfriend at the time?"

"No, I don't think so she ever talked about it, anyway."

"Do you remember the name of the psychiatrist that she talked to, and would you be willing to sign a release for us to talk to them?"

"Her name is Dr. RaNesha Jordan and if it would help my cousin then yes, I'll sign whatever I need to. Patricia was the one that I could count on when I was going through that, and we are more like sisters than we are cousins. Whatever I can do to help to get her acquitted, then I will. I also have her diary, as well. I've never opened it, but if it can help, you can have that, too."

"Thank you, Marla, for all your help. I know this wasn't easy for you to talk about, so I appreciate it. Well, let me get this back to the office. We only have a few days left before we go to trial and I still have a lot to prepare for."

"Can I see you tonight?"

"I don't think so. Terrance and I are going to be busy these next couple of days."

"Troy, is there something you're not telling me?"

"No, not at all. When I'm on a case, especially a murder case, I'm all in. That person's life is on the line and they are looking to me to see them through—I must be committed to them."

"Yea, ok," Marla snaps back.

"After this is all over, we will sit down and talk—I promise," Troy says.

Troy, now leaving Marla looks at his phone and sees that he has a missed call from Jasmine. "Hey Jasmine, what's up? I see you called. Sorry I couldn't answer; I was chasing down a lead for a case we are working on."

"Oh, nothing; I was just calling to see how your day was going, and Tre was missing his daddy."

"Oh, Tre was, huh? And what about his momma?"
"Well, his momma may have been missing you, too!"

"I miss the both of you, too."

"Are you still planning to come over tonight?" "I can if you would like me too."

"Of course."

"Is there anything you want me to bring?"

"No, I don't think so. If you want to bring some wine or something, that's fine."

"Ok, I can do that. There is also something I would like to talk to you about concerning my next move. I have had a lot of time to think today, and I know what I want to do. We can talk about that later, though; I'll let you get back to work. Oh, what would you like for dinner?"

"Whatever you cook is fine with me." "Ok, talk to you later."

"Alright, love you."

"I love you, too. Give little man a kiss for me." "I will."

Troy is now back in the office and heads straight to Terrance's office. "Hey T, I'm back and we were right—Jocelyn Aberra is her daughter, and something did happen. Marla gave us permission to talk to her daughter's psychiatrist, and she also gave me Joycelyn's diary. Hopefully, she journaled what happened. I feel a little weird about going through it, reading her thoughts as it led up to her death. Well, here goes nothing." Troy and Terrance begin reading Joycelyn's diary. "Man, you never know what our young people are going through today. It looks like we were right, though. Not only was she assaulted by Senator Johnson, but she also got pregnant. I can't even imagine having to go through that and feel like you can't talk to anyone. It's a shame to see a once vibrant young woman retreat into a shell of herself. We need to be doing more to help with mental health; our young people are dying way too fast, and for what? She did not deserve this, and how heartbreaking it was for her to feel like she couldn't talk to anyone about what was happening to her. I'm sure her mom or even her cousin would have helped her through this. Now that we know for sure the senator was a sexual predator, this will help our case. Since Joycelyn is not here, we really need to get Dr. RaNesha to verify what's in this diary. Karen, can you step in here for a minute?"

"Yes, Mr. Brooks, what can I do for you?"

"Can you call Dr. RaNesha Jordan and see if we can set up some time to talk to her about a past client? Also, can you draw up the paperwork for Marla Bordeaux, giving the doctor permission to talk to us about her client, Joycelyn Aberra?"

"Sure, I'll get on that right away."

As Troy is talking to Karen, Mike the private investigator is calling him on his cell phone with the phone number for Kimberly Russell.

"Hello, may I speak with Kimberly Russell, please?" "This is Kimberly, how can I help you?"

"Ms. Russell's, my name is Terrance Mays, from the Law offices of Brooks and Mays. The reason I'm calling you is because I have a client who is in desperate need of your help. Do you mind if I just confirm a few things with you first?"

"Sure, I guess."

"Did you ever go to Georgetown?"

"Yes, I did."

"Did you ever work for, or with, Senator Craig Johnson?"

"I did. Sir, what is this all about?"

"Well, ma'am, I'm not sure if you have heard this or not—the senator was murdered, and our client is being accused of the murder."

"Well, I'm sorry to hear that, but what does any of that have to do with me?"

"First, let me tell you that we believe our client is innocent. I can't get into the specifics of the case; however, we believe that we have a good chance to get her acquitted."

"Ok, I don't want anything to do with this. I feel bad for your client, but please leave me out of this."

"Ma'am, the reason for us calling you is that we were wondering if you had ever heard anything about the senator creating a hostile work environment, like sexual harassment or any type of unwanted advances. Whatever you can tell us would be most helpful—our client is facing life in prison, and she is a single mom."

"Look, Mr. Mays—I get it, I really do. And like I said, I feel sorry for your client, and I will be praying for her. I would appreciate it if you just left me alone. That part of me is in the past, and I don't want to go back and revisit that part of my life. I've struggled since then and now I can see the light at the end of the tunnel; that was a dark part of my life and I just want to forget it."

"I understand, I really do. And the last thing I want to do is bring back any painful memories or anything that would hurt you in any type of way—I assure you that is not our intention by reaching out to you. We are just wanting to do everything for our client that we possibly can. As I said earlier, our client is a single mom, with a young teenage daughter whose father is deceased. Would you just take down my number and if anything comes to mind, you can just call me? The trial starts on Monday this coming week, just so you know. Thank you, I appreciate you taking the time to talk to me and if I have made you feel any type of way, I apologize. Thank you again and have a blessed day."

"Sorry Troy, I stepped out because Mike got us Ms. Russell's phone number. Since you were busy, I called her and tried to convince her to tell us whatever she could about him. She didn't want to answer anything related to Senator Johnson or her time there. I left our number and told her to call if she remembered anything or had anything to tell us. I also told her the trial started on Monday. I pray she will give us a call."

"We can meet with Dr. RaNesha tomorrow at nine-thirty, unless you have something on your calendar."

"No, that will work. I think I do have an eight-thirty case, though, but that is just a quick status. I need to jump on this Zoom conference call, so I'll see you later. Before I forget, how did it go with Jasmine?"

"Man, things went great. I had a fun time with my son—playing with him on the floor and then reading to him and watching him fall asleep was priceless. Then my night with Jasmine was absolutely one for the books; she is truly the perfect woman for me. This morning she got up and cooked us all breakfast and had the kitchen clean by the time we sat down to eat—you know how funny I am about that sort of thing. I didn't say anything, though."

"Yea, I know how OCD you can be."

"Right after I left Marla's, she called just to say 'hi' then asked if I was coming over after work and what I wanted for dinner."

"Sounds like she is pulling out all the stops for you, bro!"

"Yea, looks like it—and I'm not mad at her for it, either."

"You have a good woman, my brother; hold on to her and don't let her get away again."

"Oh, that's not going to happen ever again—I have learned my lesson."

"Ok good. Well, let's get moving. I've got a date, and you have a family to come home to, too."

"I like the sound of that. Enjoy your date tonight!" "You know I will."

Jasmine and Tre are both excited to see Troy pull up in the drive, and they go to the door to greet him. "Hey, how was your day?"

"It was good—very productive. Terrance and I worked on our strategy all day. What about you and Tre?"

"We had a good day today, running errands, cleaning, and taking a nap. I've also had some time to think about what's next for me. Let's talk about this over dinner. As you know, I want to do something meaningful with my life and as I thought about what that might look like, I realized that I was already involved in and collaborating with the people that could use my help the most: the domestic violence team. I was already meeting with them and helping them write grants and what not, and giving some legal advice when I could. Now, I can open my own practice; I can hand pick my clients and truly help the community; I can give legal aid to the poor and disenfranchised."

"That's sounds like a good plan. Whatever Terrance and I can do, just let me know. My offer still stands with the office space—you can use it or come to work with us. Brooks, Mays, and Jones…it has a nice ring to it."

"Now, now—let's slow down a little bit; let's not get ahead of ourselves. I want to see what this looks like first before I make any final decisions."

"That's fair enough. I was just thinking that Terrance and I were just talking about something similar. After he told me about the statistics on people in domestic violence relationships, we knew we wanted to do something, along with mental health cases. We just didn't know what or how. So, when you started to explain what you want to do, I thought this would be perfect for you and for us."

"Hm, that does sound interesting, Mr. Brooks. Why don't I sleep on it, and we can talk about this in more detail later?"

"Sounds good to me. Why don't we finish dinner, then I will get everything cleaned up and then we can spend some time with Tre. Since you cooked this delicious meal, why don't I clean up and you go in and relax with Tre?"

"You don't know where everything is."

"I know, but if we are going to be spending more nights like this, then I need to learn."

"Well, if you insist, then who am I to stand in your way?"

"Speaking of spending more time with each other…you know starting next week my trial starts, and it's going to be a lot. I'm not sure how much time I will be able to spend here with you and Tre."

"I know, Troy, and I understand. We will make sure that you still get to spend some time with Tre. Whatever we need to do to get you all that time; now what about you and me? When will we see each other?"

"You can video call me anytime."

"You know I will be following along with the trial. I hate that we can't talk about it."

"Yea, I know, me too—I could have really used your expertise on this one.

"Well, even though I can't be there, I will be praying for you."

"I appreciate that."

"Alvin, can I speak to you for a minute?" "Sure, Matt, what's going on?"

"I wanted to check in on you to see how everything was going."

"Everything is going great. We have a solid case and I'm looking forward to going against Mr. Brooks."

"I know things have been a little difficult since we lost Jasmine and a second chair; however, Desi will be available to help you during the trial. Is there anything else you need from me?"

"No, I think I'm good."

"I'm sure I don't have to remind you that this is a very high-profile case, and you will be scrutinized extensively! People will be watching your every move and putting you under a microscope—this will either break you or elevate your career! Not to mention with Jasmine gone, there is an open seat I need to fill, and I plan on filling it right after your trial—this could be the move you have been waiting for, just so you know."

"I'm ready, Matt. I've been waiting for this for years now, and it's my time."

"Well, it's also yours to lose, Alvin." "Thanks Matt, I appreciate that."

"I'm sure we will make the right decision and choose the right man this time around! We need someone who can give this job their full attention, as well as follow direction without any attitude—if you know what I mean."

"Yes, sir, I do; I know exactly what you mean, and you don't have to worry about any of that with me. I'm all in with whatever is required of me."

"That's good to hear, Alvin. I'll let you get back to it." Alvin, full of himself now, leans back in his chair and puts his feet up on the desk as if he has arrived. Then, he picks up the phone and calls Jasmine.

"Hello Jasmine, I just wanted to call and say thank you. Thanks to you, I will be taking your spot and am next in line for the state's attorney position."

"Really Alvin, you are a piece of work. How dare you call me to gloat. I really don't care if you get the job or not. Furthermore, I'm sure you don't have the job yet and more than likely, you have yet to win this case against Troy—and without me dotting all the I's and crossing the all the T's, you may not win."

"Well, I'm sorry, did I ruffle a few feathers? Have a wonderful day and enjoy whatever it is that you're doing." Alvin hangs up the phone and holds the phone receiver in the air then pretends as if he is dropping the mic. "Take that, Ms. Jasmine Jones."

Jasmine, bewildered by Alvin's phone call, counts to ten to collect herself. "What was that?" she said to herself. "I can't believe that arrogant, pompous ass just called me.

Ugh!" She calls Troy into the room and explains what's occurred.

"Baby, don't let that small minded man get to you— he is just jealous of you and wishes he were half the lawyer you are. There will come a time when he will have to answer that phone call, and I feel sorry for him when he has to go against you in the courtroom."

"Yea, I know. I just can't believe he had the nerve to call me."

"Let him have his little fun now, because come Monday when we start this trial and by the time we are done, he won't be laughing. His time will come."

"Thanks Troy, and you're right—let the little man have his little moment and feel himself. He can laugh now, but he will cry later, as my momma used to say. How about we watch Let's Talk Live with Royce and Lisa? I heard their topic tonight is going to be good. The topic is 'Setting Priorities! Who or What should come first?'"

"That does sound interesting."

A NEW CHAPTER BEGINS

"All rise, please; court is now in session. The honorable Judge Anthony Walker presiding."

"You may be seated. Before we begin, are there any preliminaries that need to be addressed? Mr. Williams?"

"No sir, we are ready to proceed."

"Mr. Brooks?"

"No sir, we are ready to proceed, as well."

"Good, then Mr. Williams, you may proceed with your opening statement."

"Good morning, ladies and gentlemen. First, I would like to thank you for your time and your service. It is our intention to prove to you during the course of this trial that on the night in question, Ms. Patricia Henderson took a letter opener and stabbed United States Senator Craig Johnson in the neck, killing him. He was left for dead, bleeding on the floor. Now, why would she do this? We believe that she was in a jealous rage. She wanted him, and Senator Johnson—being a happily married man for over twenty years—turned her down. Things got out of control and Ms. Henderson stabbed Senator Johnson in the neck and then attempted to leave the scene without any thought of Senator Johnson lying there on the floor, bleeding out. Now, the defense will argue that it was self-defense; that somehow it was Senator Johnson who attacked Ms. Henderson, that he was the aggressor that night; that she feared for her life. Isn't that the catch phrase that we are using nowadays? Now, when you hear that, I just want you to ask yourself one simple question: Why would a sitting United States senator attack her in his own home? Where his wife and hundreds of other people were there, in his house, giving him money for his next campaign? That makes no sense! As I stated earlier, Senator Johnson was a happily married man for over twenty years. He had everything going for him; he was a shoe in to get reelected—everything was going his way. So, why would he want to do any harm to Ms. Henderson? In conclusion, when it's all said and done, you must find Ms. Patricia Henderson guilty on all counts of first-degree murder! Thank you again for your time and your service."

"Good morning, ladies, and gentlemen of the jury. I, too, would like to thank you for your time and your service. You all are playing a vital role in our justice system. My name is Troy Brooks; I am the defense council for Ms. Patricia Henderson, along with my partner, Terrance Mays, who is sitting at the table with her. Justice is what every American is looking for once they cross the courthouse doors. We believe in a system that, when it works, it's a beautiful thing—we believe that a person is innocent until proven guilty, that we all have a presumption of innocence— that is our right as an American. If you believe in our system and the way it works, then you must believe that Ms. Henderson—even though she is here in front of you all— that Ms. Henderson is still considered to be innocent until the state can prove to you otherwise. Now, Mr. Williams has already tried to convince you that this case was about jealousy; that Ms. Henderson stabbed Mr. Johnson merely because he didn't want her. Nothing could be further from the truth! In fact, it was quite the opposite. Ladies and gentlemen, Craig Johnson is a sexual predator! Who, for the past thirty-some-odd years, has been assaulting young women. On the night in question, Senator Johnson did attack Ms. Henderson and was stabbed in the neck. However, it was in self-defense—she was defending herself against a man who stood six-foot-four inches, taller than my client and at least one-hundred pounds heavier than Ms. Henderson. Ladies and gentlemen, Patricia Henderson is a single parent. She volunteers her time at the clinic for abused women. She frequently gives monies to local charities throughout the city. Her family has been, and still is, one of the biggest givers in the city. Her father has donated his time and monies to the city, as well. All the Bordeaux family has ever tried to do is be a help to anyone and everyone here in the city. The last thing I want to leave you with is this—and this is especially important—nowhere will you find any evidence that Ms. Henderson secretly or publicly ever had any type of relationship with Senator Johnson. In fact, you will find the exact opposite—she didn't even like to be in the same room as him. Now when you go back there to deliberate, I would like you to take into consideration all of the evidence and not just part of it. When we were going through the voir dire process, I asked an important question: I asked you all if you could be unbiased in the fact that this was a senator. Now we must take the title off and view him as just a normal man, the same as if he were a mechanic, schoolteacher, engineer, or what have you. Because again—when you look at all the evidence in its totality, you will see that my client is not guilty and acted in self-defense; she did what she had to do to keep from being assaulted herself. So, I am pleading with you to choose Ms. Henderson not guilty. Thank you!"

"Ladies and gentlemen of the jury, that was your opening arguments. We will now take a break and let you stretch, use the bathroom, or whatever you need to do before we get started with the trial. The bailiff will take you back now. I also want you to remember that this is not the time to talk about the case or to look for any evidence or anything of that nature. Bailiff, you can take them back now."

The courtroom clears out. Alvin, Troy, and Terrance are left in the courtroom. "Mr. Brooks, my offer of a plea deal is still on the table, if you want to quit now. You know I got this one in the bag."

"I don't think so. You are not that good, and your case isn't as solid as you think."

"Yes, well…we will see. And just so you know, I will be asking for life in prison when they find her guilty on all counts. Just like your girl couldn't manage the pressure, I don't think you can, either." Troy laughs it off and knows that Alvin is trying to get him out of character.

Terrance pulls Troy's arm. "Let's talk to our client before we do or say something we might regret."

"That's right, Mr. Mays—get your boy. You don't want to take two defeats in the same courtroom."

"Man, you are something else. We will see who wins, though. Come on Troy, let's go. He's not worth the time or energy."

"You're right, T!"

Court resumes and both sides are going at it like a heavyweight fight, exchanging jabs with each other; both attorneys are hammering witness after witness. For four days, both sides have held tough, and it looks like either side could win. Alvin is pulling no punches, hammering home his points. Troy is concerned that the jury might be persuaded because of the senator's title and the fact that the murder weapon was in the trunk, she was leaving the scene, and she had blood stains on her clothes. The state rests and Judge Walker adjourns them for the day.

"Ms. Henderson, we need to talk about your case. Let's go into the conference room. As you know we think we have a good strategy; however, I'm not sure how you feel about the case thus far. I would be remiss if I didn't tell you if I wasn't a little bit concerned with the way everything is shaping up. I know you didn't want to testify or have your daughter testify, but we may need her to tell her side of what happened that night. If she does that, I'm sure no one in their right mind could convict you for saving your daughter."

"No, no, no. I do not want my daughter to have anything to do with this trial or testifying. She has been accepted into Georgetown, and I don't want anything to interfere with that…having to answer questions about that night and making her relive those moments again…no, I will go to prison before I let that happen."

"Ms. Henderson, I understand. If I'm going to get you acquitted, then that means you and Mrs. Johnson will have to testify. We can say that he attacked you and you were defending yourself. We have pictures from that night of you with hand marks around your neck. Mrs. Johnson will be able to collaborate your story, and we can say that after she helped you fight him off, that's when the senator was stabbed which sent her into a state of shock, and that's why you left with her in the car and why you had the letter opener in your trunk. She pulled it out while you did CPR and when it didn't work, you both took off. Now we won't have to go into detail about Mrs. Johnson being physically and sexually assaulted; I believe this is the best way for us to get you acquitted. Just go home and think about it and let me know Monday morning by eight a.m. We will resume back at nine a.m. Let's go back out. and I'll ask the judge for the continuance."

"Are we ready to continue the trial, gentleman?" "The state is ready, your honor."

"Your honor, the defense respectfully asks that we wait to continue this until Monday morning at nine a.m. We have some things and witnesses that we need to move around due to scheduling conflicts and things of that nature."

"Ok, that's fine. We will start this trial back on Monday morning at nine a.m. sharp. Everyone, please be on time and ready to go. Court is adjourned."

"Ms. Henderson, please think about what I said. Go home and enjoy your weekend with your daughter. Terrance, you should have some fun as well—all of us need some time away to clear our heads and get recharged for Monday."

"True, and Troy—please take your own advice. I know you and you will be up every night working. We need you to be refreshed, as well."

Troy gets in his car and immediately video calls Jasmine. "Hey what's up? Are you busy?"

"Nothing, just sitting here getting everything situated for my new practice. How's the trial going?"

"Um, you know, it's going. The state rested today and it's still a toss-up right now. I'm praying that the jury doesn't get caught up on his title. How's Tre? I miss my little man."

"He's good, I just put him down for an afternoon nap."

"Do you mind if I come over? I miss my girl and my son."

"Not at all. In fact, I was going to ask you when you would be coming—I haven't seen you all week; I was starting to get worried."

"Oh, you were, huh? You will never have to be worried again. I'm all in when it comes to you and Tre. I am ten toes down, as they say!"

"Aw, right then, Mr. Brooks! You want me to fix you something to eat?"

"No, I'm good. In fact, I think it's time that I cooked you something—it has been awhile since I did that for you. I will stop by the store and get some groceries, and then I'll be on my way."

"Sounds good; see you soon, then."

Just as Troy enters the store, he bumps into Marla. "Hey, what are you doing here?"

"I was at the trial and needed to pick up some things from the store. I was going to invite you to dinner and give you a chance to relax. I figured you might be too tired to cook after being in trial all week. I guess I was wrong, judging by what is in your cart."

"Well, I have not been shopping in awhile, so I am just restocking my fridge."

"Are you sure? Because it looks like dinner for two."
"Yes, I am sure."

"Ok, I'm just asking because you have been different lately. If you're with someone else, just let me know—I don't want to waste my time, nor yours, if that's the case."

"Marla, as I explained to you, and you can see for yourself, this trial needs my full attention. I need to be sharp every day and not be distracted."

"If you say so, Troy!" "What does that mean?"

"Nothing. I'm just saying, Troy. If you want to just walk away, then say that."

"Marla, I really don't have time for this. I have had a long day in court arguing back and forth, and I have a lot of work preparing to tell Patricia's story—this is the last thing I want to do right now. I think we both can agree that Patricia needs my undivided attention right now. Can we not?"

"Yes, do what you must do. I guess I'll see you later, then. Enjoy the rest of your evening."

"You do the same."

The two go their separate ways while Troy takes a deep sigh of relief. Marla is fuming. She can sense that something is off with Troy, and he is not telling her something—this is the second time she has seen him and he didn't approach her for a hug or a kiss—nothing. He just walks away as if nothing ever happened between the two of them.

"Hey, Jasmine, I'm on my way to the house. Is there anything that you need me to do before I get there?"

"No, just come on."

"Ok, do you mind if I park in the garage?" "No, I don't mind. What's going on, though?"

"I ran into Marla at the store, and she started to question me about why I hadn't been spending much time with her and if there was someone else."

"What did you say to that?"

"I told her that I had to stay focused on the trial and that is where my thoughts are right now. As soon as this trial is over, I will let her know that we can't be together."

"Are you sure that is what you want? She is rich, smart, and pretty—she could give you everything you could ever want or need."

"Yea, she could give me a lot, but there are two things that she can never give me. First thing is, she could never give me the type of love that you give me—you bring peace to my life, a burning desire to want to be better in every way possible. You make me want to wake up in the morning and take on the day with a new perspective. You give me something to look forward to and not just going through the motions. Then, there is our beautiful son Tre, that is a blessing and unspeakable joy—you both are all I need or want, and that to me is priceless."

"You are all we want, too, Troy. Thanks love!"

Monday morning comes around, and it feels like they just left the courtroom. Troy is feeling refreshed and ready to take on the world. He and Terrance meet in the conference room right outside of the courtroom.

"Hey, T have you seen Patricia out there?" "No, I didn't see her."

"Well, it's still early yet. I'm sure she will be here, though. What do you think she is going to do?"

"I don't know yet; I hope she allows us to do our job. If there was any other way, I could get her off with an acquittal, I would—but this is our best and only option."

"I agree; let's just hope that she does, too."

Just then. Patricia knocks on the conference room door.

"May I come in?"

"Yes, of course you can. Have you thought about what we discussed?"

"I have thought of nothing else, and I trust you. If you feel this is our best way to move forward, then I will go with that."

"Are you sure? Because Alvin is going to come after you hard; he is going to grill you with everything he has. Are you ready for that?"

"Yes, I'm ready."

"Good. Anytime you feel yourself getting anxious or upset, just take a breath, calm your spirit. Once you do that, speak clearly and just be you; allow the jury to see who Patricia Henderson is—the kind and caring mother, the person who gives selfishly to others with her time and talents; the one who would do anything for anybody. Show them the Christ in you!"

Troy first calls Mrs. Johnson to the stand. "For the record, would you state your full name and spell your last name."

"My name is Michelle Johnson; J-O-H-N-S-O-N." "Were you married to Senator Craig Johnson?" "Yes, I was."

"How long were the two of you married?" "Over twenty years."

"Do you know my client, Ms. Patricia Henderson,

a.k.a Patricia Bordeaux?" "Yes."

"How do you know her?"

"We met some years ago at a domestic violence shelter."

"Were you a speaker or coordinator there?" "No."

"Then why would you be there?"

"I was a victim of domestic violence."

"Mrs. Johnson, I know this may be painful for you to relive; however, I have to ask you: What made you go to the shelter and who was the perpetrator?"

"It was my husband, Senator Craig Johnson."

"You honor, I object," shouts Alvin. "Senator Johnson is not on trial here."

"No, he is not—but you opened the door when you asked about the so-called affair with my client. We are just establishing their relationship."

"Overruled. You can continue, Mr. Brooks." "Thank you. Mrs. Johnson, you were about to tell us about why you were at the shelter."

"I met Craig right before he became senator, when he was still working on the city council. Things started off great. However, the closer we got to the election, the meaner he got and one day, I said something that he didn't like about a campaign poster or something like that. The next thing I knew, he was backhanding me, and I woke up with swollen eyes. He apologized and said he would never do it again. I forgave him and stayed with him. It wasn't too much longer after that we were at an event. We drove separate cars that night and when I arrived, he didn't like the outfit I had on, so he made me go back home. When he came home that night after being out drinking all night, he beat me up badly. I somehow managed to get away and found my way to the shelter—which is where I met Patricia officially for the first time."

"What do you mean officially?"

"I used to go to their fundraisers whenever Craig couldn't or didn't want to go. He would send me in his place, since I was his personal assistant. So, I would see Patricia, but we never really met. On the night I went to the shelter, she was the first person I met. She seemed like she understood what I was going through, so it made it easier to talk to her. She was genuine and caring—we would talk for hours while I was there. Eventually, we became friends."

"How long did you stay at the shelter?"

"I was there for a couple of weeks—three or four at the most."

"Did you ever tell Patricia who was your assailant?"

"No, I never told anyone. I was too embarrassed to say anything."

"How did you end up leaving the shelter?"

"In one of my weaker moments, I reached out to Craig, and he convinced me to meet him, so I did. We talked and once again, he promised not to hit me anymore and he would go to counseling. I was still on the fence when he pulled out this ring and proposed. I really thought he had changed, so I just left with him and never went back to the shelter. After that, I didn't see Patricia until the night of the party."

"Before we get to that night, can you tell us a little about your marriage?"

"It was pure hell. There were daily beatings when he felt like it. He cheated on me all the time. He would come home with perfume on his shirts or lipstick on his collars, and there was always an excuse of how he had hugged someone or some other BS story."

"No further questions at this time, your honor; but I would like to recall her later."

"Mr. Williams, your witness."

"Mrs. Johnson—first, let me give my condolences at the loss of your husband. You stated that you and Ms. Henderson became friends, is that correct?"

"Yes, we did."

"Are you still friends today?" "Yes, I would say so."

"As her friend, you wouldn't want to see her go to prison, would you?"

"No, I wouldn't want to see her go to prison."

"Would it be safe to say that you would lie for her?" "No, I wouldn't lie for her."

"No further questions, your honor." "Redirect, Mr. Brooks?"

"Yes, your honor. Mrs. Thompson, did you see your husband choking Ms. Henderson?"

"Yes, I did."

"Did you see your husband beating on Ms. Henderson?"

"Yes, I did!"

"No further questions, your honor."

"The witness may now step down. Mr. Brooks, your next witness."

"Your honor, I'd like to call my client, Ms. Patricia Henderson. Ms. Henderson, can you state your full name and spell your last name?"

"My name is Patricia Henderson. H-E-N-D-E-R-S-O-N."

"Would you mind if I called you Patricia?" "No, that's fine."

"Patricia, how did you come to know Senator Craig Johnson?"

"I first met him through my father, Roy Bordeaux. My father loved politics and always did whatever he could to help young minority politician's raise money for their campaigns. Senator Johnson would always come over to the house."

"Did something happen one night when he came over to the house?"

"Yes!"

"Can you tell us what happened?"

Patricia pauses, her eyes begin to tear up, and a lump starts to swell in her throat. The scent from his cologne that day is still in her nostrils. She clinches her hands together and takes a deep breath. "One day, he came over to the house."

"Who is he?"

"Senator Johnson. He came over to talk to my father and I told him he wasn't home. He didn't care—he tried to push up on me. I told him no and that I would tell my father. He said he didn't care and that no one would believe me because of who he was, and that if I did, it would make my father look bad. He then proceeded to rape me. There was nothing I could do—he was so strong, so all I could do was lay there."

"Patricia, do you need a minute?"

"No, I'm good." Tears are now flowing like a waterfall.

"Take a second and gather yourself. What did you do next?"

"After he was finished, he got up like nothing had happened. He got up and got dressed, then told me that I better not tell anyone and walked out. I sat there for a while in shock, and then I took a shower and tried to wash the stench of him off me—the more I scrubbed, the more I smelled his cheap cologne."

"Did you ever see him again after that day?"

"Yes, I saw him several more times after that. I would never stay in the same room with him, though; I would always make up some excuse to leave so that I wouldn't have to see his face."

"Patricia, I'm sorry you had to go through that. I know this next question may be difficult for you to think about, so if you need to take a break or anything, just let me know. Now, on the night in question: Can you tell us what happened in your own words?"

"Well at first, I didn't want to go to the event because I knew Senator Johnson would be there, but after talking to my therapist, she suggested that I go in order to get past my pain, and the only way to do that is to be in the same room with him and eventually confront my past. So, this would be a good opportunity to do that. When I first arrived at the event, I didn't see him, which eased my nerves. When I finally did, it was about an hour into the event when they called everyone into the gathering room to make an announcement there—he was smiling and wearing what looked like the same dark suit with the red tie that he assaulted me in."

"Your honor, I object. The senator is not the one on trial here, and this assassination of my client's character should be stricken from the record."

"Sustained! Move on, Ms. Henderson."

"Ms. Henderson, what happened next?" Troy chimes in.

"When I saw him standing there, all that pain and hurt that I had in me came rushing back like a tidal wave— it was like that night happening all over again. So, I walked out to the balcony to get some air and to calm my nerves. When I came back in, I saw him heading toward his office and I decided to confront him. When I called his name, he first pretended that he didn't hear me. I called out his name again and this time I got his attention. He stopped at the door to his office, and I asked him if he remembered me. He said that he didn't, and that he meets so many people that it's hard to keep everyone straight. I then told him that my name was Patricia Bordeaux when I was a teenager; he then told me that he did remember me. I then asked him if he remembered what he did to me when I was a young teen. At first, he tried to deny that it happened and that I must have him mixed up with someone else. Then, I told him who my father was, and he knew then—he grabbed my arm and pulled me into his study. 'Get in here,' he yelled at me through his teeth. He starts to scold me, as if I were a child. We began going back and forth about what he did—he continues to deny it and then he slaps me across the face. We then began to fight. We traded blows for a minute and then the next thing I knew, he was on top of me with his hands around my throat and right before I blacked out, he let go. At first, I didn't know why, then I saw him, and Michelle tussling and he had her pinned on the wall. I grab him to pull him off her and we start going at it all over again. I remember falling back into the desk and he started choking me again. As he was choking me again, I reached all over the desk trying to find something to hit him with, to get him to let go of me. I finally grabbed a letter opener that was laying on his desk and I swung it, hitting him in the neck. There was so much blood oozing out of him that I didn't know what to do; I could hear him gurgling and choking on his blood. Once I gathered myself, I tried to help him, so I grabbed the knife, pulling it out of his neck, and tried to give him CPR. Before you knew it, he was gone. Michelle and I both stood there frozen in time for what seemed to be like hours but was only a few minutes. Michelle stood there frozen. I tried to get her to snap out of it and I had no luck. I then told her to gather her things so we could go. At this point, neither one of us was thinking clearly. We just wanted out of there, to get away to breathe, to collect our thoughts and gather our composure. I ended up driving to a local hotel. I got out of the car and booked the room. Michelle, still catatonic in the car, stayed in until I came back and walked her to the room. After I dropped her off, I was driving back to the event because the shelter was receiving an award, and that's when I was pulled over and they noticed some blood on my clothing."

"Ms. Henderson would it be fair to say that you didn't mean to harm Senator Johnson that night?"

"I truly had no intention of harming him—things just got out of hand once he slapped me. I just wanted to confront him and let him know how he hurt me."

"One last question. Ms. Henderson, would it be safe to say that you were only defending yourself from being choked when you stabbed him with the letter opener?"

"Yes, that's exactly what it was. He had already choked me to the point where I was about to lose consciousness—I didn't know how far he would take it the second time, so I did anything I could to get free."

"Thank you, Ms. Henderson. I have no more questions for you."

"Your witness, Mr. Williams."

"Ms. Henderson, may I call you Patricia?" "Yes, that's fine."

"Are you ok? Do you need a break or anything?" "No, I'm fine."

"Ok, can you tell us again how you know Senator Johnson?"

"We met years ago. He was one of my father's mentees."

"If he were a mentee of your father, would it be safe to say, in your opinion, that your father thought he was a good person?"

"I have no idea what my father thought of him."

"Before the day you say he allegedly attacked you, did you think he was a good man?"

"I guess I don't remember what I thought of him when I was a kid—I only knew what I saw, like most people."

"What do you think most people see?" "How do I know what others see?"

"Well, I'm just going off what you said. Do you think most people see a good man, a loving devoted husband, a hero of the people, an unselfish man who puts his community before himself? Is that what most people see, Ms. Henderson?"

"I don't know what most people see, nor do I care. I'm sure he hasn't sexually assaulted most people, either."

"Did anyone see this alleged incident?" "No, of course not!"

"Did you ever tell anyone about what allegedly happened?"

"No, I was embarrassed, and I didn't want to embarrass my father."

"So, no one saw it! You didn't tell anyone, and now you want us to believe that a sitting United States senator sexually assaulted you when you were a teenager, and all these years later you confront him and get into an intense argument, and he attacks you and you stab him? Is that what you really want us to believe?"

"That's what happened!"

"Now Patricia, you said when you saw him all these old feelings came running back to you, is that correct?"

"Yes!"

"Was one of those old feelings anger or rage?" "Yes."

"What about hurt?" "Yes!"

"Would it be safe to say that you wanted to hurt him like he had hurt you?"

"Mr. Williams, I know what you're trying to do, and although he did what he did, I didn't want to kill him, nor did I want to hurt him—I just wanted him to know that he no longer had any power over me, and I wanted him to see and know that I am a survivor."

"You mean to tell me that you finally see the man who allegedly attacked you as a teen, and you don't want to hurt him as much as he hurt you? Come on, Ms. Henderson! May I remind you that you are under oath here?"

"When it first happened, yes, I wanted him to feel that same hurt; that same pain that I felt—and even for the moment when I first saw him, I had thoughts of hurting him. Then once I stepped outside and got some air, I thought about my baby, and that was enough to snap me back into my reality. I taught my daughter that when someone hurts you, the best way to get them back is to keep moving forward and to never allow anyone to take your power away from you. People can take many things, but they can never take your power. Unless you give it to them. Once I realized that about myself, then all the hidden feelings I had about that night with the senator went away, and I was able to see the senator and confront him about what he did to me."

"That's fine, Ms. Henderson, and I'm happy to hear that you got your power back; but as you were getting your power back, the senator was losing his power because you stabbed him. You were mad at what he did to you all those years ago, and you got into an intense argument; one thing led to another, and you stabbed him, didn't you? You wanted him to pay for what he did all those years ago, isn't that right? Ms. Henderson, admit it: you hated him for what he did to you, and you killed him, right?"

"No, that's not right, Mr. Williams. I knew Senator Johnson would get what he had coming eventually, on this side or the other."

"So, you decided that he would get it on this side, right, Ms. Henderson?"

"I object your honor!" "Sustained; move on, council."

"Ms. Henderson, tell us this: If you're innocent and this was self-defense, then why did you leave? Why not stay, or better yet, call the police and let them know what happened? Innocent people do not flee the scene of a murder."

"I don't know, I guess we both panicked and were in shock."

"You're telling me that you were so panicked and in shock that you could get your car but not make a phone call? Come on, Ms. Henderson, tell the truth—you left because you killed him in cold blood. You were angry and wanted revenge for the pain that he allegedly caused you and you stabbed him."

"No, that's not what happened! I…I…I…" "You what, Ms. Henderson?"

"I…I didn't want him dead; I didn't mean to hurt him. He was going to kill me. He had his hands around my neck."

"Your honor, can we take a small break and allow my client to regain her composure?"

"Yes, let's do that. We have been going at it since nine a.m. and it is now eleven-thirty a.m. Let's take a recess now and come back at one p.m. Ms. Henderson, you can step down; court is now in recess."

"Ms. Henderson, let's find a quiet place to talk. I'm not going to lie to you—right now, this jury could go either way. You did good on the stand all the way up to the end. However, this one question has been on my mind and Mr. Williams hit it right on the head. Why didn't you call the police or stay until they got there?"

"I panicked and we were scared."

"Scared of what, though? The senator was dead. He couldn't hurt you anymore. Ms. Henderson, are you telling me everything? You're facing a lot of prison time and I need to know everything that happened so that I can help you. If you're holding something from me, I need to know."

Patricia drops her head and begins to sob. "That night when Senator Johnson died, I had heard that my daughter was there, so when I came back from getting some air, I went looking for her and I ended up walking into his office and saw her with her shirt ripped open, and he was trying to get on top of her. I ran in and tried to get him off her. That's when we got into it and he started choking me for the first time. As he was choking me, that's when Michelle came in looking for him, and she saw the senator on top of me she pulled him off me. They get into it and once I come back to myself, I engage him again; he starts choking me again and that's when I stabbed him. I didn't want to tell you that part because I didn't want my daughter to be involved. Senator Johnson is her father, and no one knows it. Back when he raped me eighteen years ago, I got pregnant. I have never told anyone that he was the father until now—you guys are the only two that know. That's why I have been trying to keep my daughter out of this whole thing; I didn't want her to have to relive this whole ordeal answering questions or God forbid she finds out that she was conceived due to rape, and that her father is a sexual predator who was also had attacked her—she has too much going for her and a bright future ahead of her."

"Well, how did she come to be working for the Senator?"

"She was doing something for extra credit, that is all I know."

"Now it all makes sense." "What's that supposed to mean?"

"Well, while we were doing our investigation, we found out that her cousin also worked for the senator as an intern.

We believe that he raped her as well and she ended up pregnant—that is why she committed suicide. The senator must have been using his contacts at Georgetown to send him a certain type of young women to come and intern for him, because we found at least two other women that went to Georgetown and interned for him."

"Are you serious?"

"Yes! Now, we have some decisions to make and not a whole lot of time to make them. The first one is what do we do about your daughter being there? I know you don't want her involved in this; however, she is, and this may be our best defense. The jury consists of mostly women who will be sympathetic to you—they will understand that a mother would do anything to protect her child!"

"No, absolutely not! I would rather go to prison than see her brought into this and hurt by what she could have to go through with the reporters and being grilled on the stand—and not to mention finding out who her father is. No, that's just too much!"

"I get it, Patricia; I really do. I would just feel more at ease if we could give the jury more, because right now it's about fifty-fifty on what the jury will decide. Hopefully, the photos of your bruised neck will be enough to persuade them."

"You have done a brilliant job, Troy, and now I need you to do one thing for me."

"Thank you. What can I do for you?"

"I need you to believe—to have faith that the Lord will see us through. That he will not leave us nor forsake us. The truth will prevail, Troy; we just have to believe. Now, you're a believer, right?"

"Yes ma'am, I am."

"Then just let the Lord lead you. When you give your closing arguments, speak from your heart. Ask the Lord to speak to you and to speak through you, so that when the jury sees you, they see the God in you."

"I can do that. As for that last question—why did you leave? Take a breath and just answer the question. If you don't know, then just say that. Are you ready?"

"Yes, I'm as ready as I can be."

"Ms. Henderson, before we took our break, I had asked you why you would run if you did nothing wrong."

"I'm not sure why we ran. As I stated earlier, we panicked and just took off."

"Didn't you know it would be wrong to leave the scene of a crime?"

"Yes, I knew that. I also knew how it would look."
"How is that?"

"All some people will see is this facade of the senator— you even alluded to it earlier. They see this man who does charity work, gives money to the poor, this political figure. When behind closed doors he is a wife beater, a cheater, a liar, a pedophile, and a rapist."

"Your honor, I object!"

"You asked the question, counselor. Overruled." "No more questions, your honor."

"Mr. Brooks, do you have any more questions?"

"Yes, your honor; I do have two more questions. Ms. Henderson, do you recall me asking you why you were afraid that night? Would you like to elaborate on that a little further? Could it be that you were afraid of just what is taking place right now?"

"Yes sir. I have never been in trouble for anything a day in my life; I have never had any run-ins with the police, period. I just panicked."

"Ms. Henderson, one last question. When you stabbed Senator Johnson, were you just defending yourself?"

"Absolutely! I thought he was going to kill me. He had already choked me to the point where I felt like I was about to pass out, and I didn't know what he would do this time. I only wanted him to let me go."

"Is there anything else you would like to let this jury know?"

"Yes. As much as I disliked the senator for what he did to me, I would never wish death upon him. What he did to me was horrible; however, with the help of the Lord and my therapist, I moved on. Do I still think about it? Of course, I do—that is something that will never leave me. The thought of him violating me and then dismissing it as if I were nothing; as if I were just a piece of trash that he used and then just discarded. Something like that never leaves you. You can't just forget that, but you can move past it, especially when you have someone that needs you—so that's what I have focused on and dedicated myself to."

"Ms. Henderson, who would that be?"

"My daughter, Shay. She is a senior in high school with a 4.0 GPA and has now been accepted into Georgetown to become a lawyer. She is a very bright and beautiful girl, with a lot of potential."

"That's it, your honor; no more questions." "Mr. Brooks, does the defense rest?"

"Yes, we do, your honor. Thank you!"

"Mr. Williams; Mr. Brooks—are you ready for closing arguments or do you need a few minutes to get your thoughts together?"

"Yes, I'm ready your honor." "I'm ready, also, your honor."

Alvin Williams goes first with his closing argument; he carefully and very skillfully lays out what he believes took place. He is a highly skilled and charismatic orator and knowing that he has a fifty percent chance of winning this case, he is laying it on extra thick, using everything that he learned in law school and the last ten years of being a trial court lawyer. He also knows that he has a lot riding on this conviction—moving up in the ranks in the state attorney's office, as well as the media attention he would receive which would bolster his future political career. When he finishes, he turns and looks at Troy with a smug, confident look and a little smirk, as if to say, "top that if you can," and he takes his seat.

Troy is up next, and before he gets up out of his seat, Patricia leans over to whisper in his ear. "Don't forget what I said—be yourself and let the Lord use you. I trust you!" Troy takes a sip of water and adjusts his tie. He knows this is his last chance to convince the jury that Patricia is innocent. As he gets ready to address the jury, he says a small prayer to himself and then begins to speak. Every word is calculated, every sentence carefully constructed and put together. Troy is like one of the great painters putting words to canvas to paint a picture, telling the jury exactly what they needed to know, to the point they could almost see the events of the night unfolding as if it played like a movie. He uses his voice like a master musician to invoke feelings in each and every one of the jurors to gain sympathy for Patricia. Alvin is getting nervous watching Troy work the room and the jurors; he knows that if he is going to win, it's going to take his second closing and a miracle in order to get a conviction. Troy has everyone in the courtroom eating out the palm of his hands and hanging on to every syllable that comes out of his mouth. —everything that you would want your lawyer to do and say is being displayed from Troy. He is humble, clear, precise, believable, and everything he has said is done with perfect precision. As he closes his final statement, he looks at Patricia and he can see that she is pleased with his closing; he glances to the back of the courtroom and there in the corner of the room is Jasmine, sitting and watching. His heart is full, and a tear falls from his eye. He finishes with: "ladies and gentlemen, when you go back into the jury room to deliberate, put yourself in Ms. Henderson's shoes for just a moment and ask yourself what you would have done if it were you. Here is a man that not only beat up his wife to the point both of her eyes were swollen shut and her ribs broken; he also had raped you as a teenager, then on the night all of this happened, he choked you—not once, but twice—to the point you almost blacked out. Imagine someone with their hands around your neck, squeezing the life out of you and there is nothing you can do about it, because he is so much stronger than you and you're fighting for breath and you're reaching for anything you can find to get him to stop. As your feeling around on the desk, you feel something that can help you, so you pick it up and swing it. At that moment in time, your self-defense mechanism kicks in and you do what you must do to save your life. I just ask that you remember that when you're back there deliberating and choose not guilty on all counts. Thank you very much for your time and for serving on this jury."

As Troy prepares to take his seat, he looks back at Jasmine; she winks and gives him a nod of approval. Troy sits and Patricia leans over to tell him how grateful she is for what he had just done. "No matter what this jury decides, Troy, you have done a wonderful job, and I will be forever grateful for what you have done."

"You're more than welcome." Terrance slides him a note that says: "You are the man!" They bump fists and await Alvin's retort.

"Mr. Williams, you get the last word."

Alvin stands and tries to speak but his voice cracks. "Excuse me." He tries again and a lump swells in his throat; sweat begins to start forming on his forehead. Alvin takes out a handkerchief from his jacket pocket to wipe his brow and takes a deep breath to gain his composure. He starts over and does the best he can to deliver his rebuttal argument. Alvin cuts it short to keep from digging himself in a hole even further; he prays that his first argument would be good enough to get a conviction. He then thanks the jury for their service and takes a seat. It is now out of his control and up to the jury to decide what happens next. This time, when he goes to his seat there is no smug smirk, no smile—nothing.

"Ladies and gentlemen of the jury, you have now heard testimony from both sides and now it's time for you to go back and deliberate. Bailiff, you can take them back to the jury room so they can deliberate."

THE VERDICT

"What do we do now, Mr. Brooks?"

"Now, Ms. Henderson, we pray and we wait for the jury to come back with a verdict. Sometimes they will have a question if they are unsure about something. When they do have a verdict or question, the bailiff will call my cell phone and let us know."

"If I am found guilty, will I be taken into custody right away or will they give me some time to say my goodbyes?"

"That all depends on the judge. Since you're not a flight risk, I will ask the judge to give you some time to get your affairs in order and give us a future sentencing date. Let's think positive, though—you will be found not guilty on all counts and we won't have to worry about a sentencing date, and we can put all this behind us. Shay can go off to college and become great, and you can go live your life and enjoy your next…whatever that might be. One thing that I have learned about you, Ms. Patricia Henderson, is that you have spent most of your life trying to help other people and giving to others with no thought of yourself. You have done a wonderful job with that, and now it's time to be a little selfish and feel good about it. Find something that you have always wanted to do and do it—or if you want to, just take some time and get some much-needed rest and relaxation. Sit on a beach, have a glass of wine, and just listen to the water as it rolls up on the beach." Whatever you decide to do, just do it for you! If you don't take care of you then who will. Self-care is to often overlooked as being selfish when in fact it's just the opposite,

"Alvin, what was that? Were you trying to lose this case?"

"What are you talking about, Matt?"

"That second closing of yours—if you can even call it that—was terrible! You choked and that's putting it nicely."

"I didn't think it was that bad."

"Not that bad? Are you kidding me?"

"Matt, calm down. We got this in the bag; the jury loved me. That second closing may not have been my finest work, but I killed them with the first one. I perfectly laid out the facts of this case and had them eating out of my hand— they were hanging on my every word. We have motive, the murder weapon, and her leaving the scene; this case is in the bag.”

“Oh, you think so?”

“Of course, I do. It would not surprise me if this jury didn’t have a verdict in less than an hour—I’m that confident in the case that I put on. True Mr. Brooks did fairly good, and his closing was ok; however, I gave them undisputable proof. All he did was slander the senator’s name and reputation.”

“I hope you’re right, because the mayor is going to have my behind for lunch, and if that happens, you know what they say about it rolling downhill when the stuff hits the fan; it’s not going to be nice. Oh, and that promotion you have been looking to get? You can forget about it.”

“Matt, relax; trust me. We are going to get a guilty verdict!”

“Hey Jasmine, just thought I would call and say thank you for being there for my closing. I appreciate the support.”

“No problem; I know how important this is and although we thought it would be best if I stayed away from this case, I wanted you to know that I’m here for you—that closing you did was one for the ages. You nailed it and gave that jury every reason for a not guilty verdict!”

“Thank you, Jasmine, I really appreciate it. That’s high praise coming from you. I pray you’re right.”

“Well, after listening to you lay out what happened, if I were on that jury, I would definitely vote not guilty.”

“Well, I guess we will see. What’s Tre doing? I miss my little man.”

"He's good. He is in there napping. He has had quite a busy morning running and playing with that basketball hoop you bought him; that ball has been in his hands ever since you gave it to him."

"We might just have the next Black Mamba on our hands. Wouldn't that be something?"

"I wouldn't be mad at it, that's for sure."

"Yea, me either. Did you get all your paperwork together to get the ball rolling for your own practice?"

"Yes, I did, but we can talk about that later when your case is over."

"Ok, that's fine. We can celebrate my winning this case and your new beginning."

"That would be lovely, and it gives me something I can look forward to tonight."

"In that case, why don't I give you something else to look forward to?"

"Hm, I like the way you think. You make me want to come home right now."

"I wish you were here; it will be worth the wait, though—when you get here and we celebrate."

"Terrance, Troy, how do you guys do this? It's been three hours and nothing. No verdict, no questions, nothing. This is driving me crazy."

"I fully understand Patricia—I know it's not easy, and you just have to stay focused on your future and your daughter's future—what it will be like to see her when she graduates from college; when she gets married and has kids—that type of thing."

"Hang on one second. Hello, this is Troy Brooks."

"This is Judge Walker's bailiff, Dewayne. We have a verdict. Are you close to the courthouse?"

"Yes, I'm about five minutes away; I can be right there."

"Ok, we will see you soon."

"Hello, Mr. Williams, this is Dewayne, the bailiff. We have a verdict. You can come back to the courtroom now."

"All rise! Court is now in session; the honorable Judge Anthony Walker presiding."

"You can be seated. Mr. Williams, Mr. Brooks; my bailiff, informs me that we have a verdict. Are both of you ready to proceed?"

"Yes, your honor," they both reply.

"Dewayne, you can bring in the jury. Ladies and gentlemen in the gallery: I want to remind you that when the verdict is read, there will be no loud outburst either way the verdict goes. We will conduct ourselves respectfully on both sides. I hope I am clear.

"Will the foreperson please rise? Have you reached a verdict?"

"Yes, we have your honor."

"Will you please hand it to my bailiff?" Dewayane takes the papers with the verdict on it. Judge Walker reads it and hands it back to Dewayne to give to the foreperson.

"Ms. Henderson, will you please rise. Mr. foreperson, would you please read the verdict aloud?"

"We the jury in case 22CF4237 find the defendant not guilty!"

"Ladies and gentlemen of the jury, I want to personally thank you for your service in this case. I know it was not easy to make a decision; however, I want you to know that on behalf of both attorneys and myself, we appreciate your time. You may now be excused from your duties as a juror. Bailiff, you can take them back for the last time and I'll be back there in a few minutes to talk to you all and answer any questions if you have any."

When the verdict is read, Ms. Henderson is overcome with emotion and bursts into tears while thanking God. Troy and Terrance help her to her seat, then hug each other and shake hands.

"You did it man! You did it! That closing argument you gave was so powerful; I knew they would find her not guilty."

"No, Terrance—we did it. I couldn't have done this without you, my brother. We are a team. Ms. Henderson, let's get out of here and go celebrate."

"Before we go, I want to thank you both for what you have done for me and my baby girl. I know I wasn't the easiest client to work with and Troy, the way you let GOD use you at the end was something to see and to hear. The people saw and heard your heart. I feel so relieved to finally tell someone what happened to me all those years ago; it is like a weight off my shoulders. I finally feel free of the shame and the hurt that has been haunting me for years."

Just as Patricia is finishes her thank you, Marla walks up from behind Troy. "Well done, Mr. Brooks, and congrats to you, cousin—I'm so happy for you!" Marla and Patricia hug.

"Thank you, Marla, for hiring them. They were magnificent."

"You're welcome, Patricia; and yes, they were. Troy, can I speak to you for a minute alone, please?"

"Yea, sure; what's up?"

"Well, now that the trial is over, I was thinking we could have a late dinner, some drinks, and then go back to my place."

"I'm sorry Marla; it's been a long day and I am exhausted. This has taken a lot out of me, and I just want to go home and decompress for a minute and then go to bed. We can talk later."

"Troy, what is going on? You have been avoiding me for some time now, and I'm not going to keep waiting. I've explained to you that if you have someone else, then just let me know and I can move on with my life and not chase you around or beg you for some of your time."

"You know, Marla, at this point in time I think that it would be best if we just went our separate ways. I'm going to be honest—I'm still in love with my ex and I'm hoping that we can work it out. Until I know for sure if we are going to try again, that's where my focus is going to be. I don't want to waste any of your time, and I certainly don't want you to feel that you have to chase me around for my time. I'm sorry to have wasted any of your time. Like I was saying, I'm tired and I just want to go home, relax, and get a good night's sleep."

"Are you freaking kidding me, Troy Brooks? You have been playing with my feelings this whole time. I knew you had been acting funny for some reason—you were just using me the whole time. I thought you were different than all these other guys out here playing the field."

"Marla, I assure you that's not the case."

"I don't need your assurances; I'm not stupid—I know when I'm being played and you're playing me. I have already told you that if it was someone else, then just tell me. You could have told me this weeks ago."

"Marla, I really didn't know when you asked. After seeing what Patricia was facing and how her life could have potentially changed for the rest of her life, I realized that our time here is short and we have to do whatever we can while we can; and right now, that is what would make me happy. I can't move on with you or anyone else until that is resolved in my mind and in my heart. I hope you understand."

"Yea, I understand—I understand that you lied to me. Whatever, though! I am done with you! Please don't ever call me again, Mr. Brooks, I don't ever want to see you again." Marla storms out of the courthouse.

"Troy, are you alright? I saw Marla storm out of here and she was pissed."

"Yea, I'm ok. I told her that it wasn't going to work out between us and that my head and heart still belonged to my ex, and that I was going to try to work it out with her."

"Wow, no wonder she was so upset. Her and Jasmine don't like each other, right?"

"Right. I didn't tell her it was Jasmine, though."

"Yea, that was probably a good idea—she might have made a scene. Troy, you did it. I have to be honest, when we first took this case and she didn't want to talk to you, I thought there is no way we can win this case and this woman was going to prison for a long time. I'm so glad that things worked out for her and her daughter."

"Yea, me too. What are you getting ready to do now?"

"I'm going to go grab a bottle of wine, sit on the couch, and just hang out with Jasmine and Tre. It feels like I haven't seen them in about a month. What about you?"

"I think I'm going to go to Club A and celebrate." "Oh, yeah; is Lisa going with you?"

"No, she's out of town on business. Enjoy your night and I'll give you a call tomorrow."

"Cool, sounds good." Troy could not wait to get outside of the courthouse to call Jasmine to tell her the good news.

"Hey love, we did it! The jury voted not guilty, can you believe it?!"

"Yes, I can believe it—that closing you did might have been the best I've ever heard. You were so convincing—the way you put everything together was masterful. You have a way with words, Mr. Brooks," says Jasmine.

"Thank you, that means a lot coming from you." "Where are you?"

"I was on my way to the store and then I'll be over. Oh yea, I had a conversation with Marla today after the verdict was in. She wanted me to go out to dinner with her and when I told her no, she flipped out. I explained to her that my mind and my heart was with my ex, and that I was going to pursue a relationship with her. She then told me that she never wanted to see or hear from me again."

"Really? Did you tell her that it was me that you were pursuing?"

"No, I didn't; I just said my ex. I didn't want to get her even more riled up than she already was."

"How do you feel about that?"

"I'm good. I knew early on that something was off about her and that I couldn't see us having a future together. She always seemed pushy and there was always something that just didn't seem right."

"What happened after you told her that?"

"She just stormed off out of the courthouse—all I can say is goodbye and good riddance to her. Well, I'm pulling up now."

"Ok."

"Oh, my goodness—there is nothing I like better than coming home to you and Tre, and you greeting me at the door with a hug and a kiss; this is truly a wonderful way to celebrate a victory and see justice done."

"Now that, counselor, I can surely agree." "Where is Tre?"

"He's in his room sleeping."

"Sleep huh? Why don't we skip dinner and just go straight for dessert?"

"Oh, Mr. Brooks; I like the way you think." Jasmine and Troy spend the rest of the day in each other's arms and playing with Tre.

"Good morning, my love."

"Good morning, I can't believe I slept so late." "Yea, I can't either; but when you were not up at the

crack of dawn, I knew you were tired, so I just let you sleep."

"I guess I haven't gotten much sleep the past couple of weeks because of the trial."

"Well, now that the trial is behind you, I wanted to talk to you about your offer."

"Oh, yea; what's up?"

"I was hoping that if your offer is still good for me to use some space in your office, I could start my own practice and focus it on domestic violence, getting the men and women of this community some type protection from domestic violence. I also want to do family law."

"Jasmine, I think that's wonderful. You will be really good at that, and our community could really use this and you. Whatever you need from Terrance and I, just let us know."

"Shouldn't we at least call Terrance and let him know what we are thinking? I mean, we do want to do things decently and in order."

"Yea, I guess you're right. I'll call him right now." "Hey T, what's up, man? Were you busy?"

"No, just sitting here watching tv and eating breakfast."

"The reason I'm calling so early is that Jasmine and I were just talking about her next move, and she wants to start her own practice. She wants to focus on domestic violence and family law."

"Really? That's wonderful! We were just talking about expanding and doing more in the community, so that would be great. Does she want to work with us?"

"That's the idea if you're cool with it."

"Of course I am; she is a brilliant attorney, so this would be great."

"We were hoping that you felt that way." "When does Jasmine want to start?" "She said Monday, if that's cool."

"Yes, that's fine with me."

"Ok, we will see you on Monday, then."

"Aw right, my brother I'll see you both on Monday morning. Now tell the new attorney they have to bring doughnuts in on their first day at the office."

Troy laughs, "I sure will. Have a good day, man." "You do the same!"

"Well, it's official, Jasmine: the space is yours and you can get started Monday. One thing though—you have to bring doughnuts for the office on Monday."

"Oh, I think I can handle that."

"You know Jasmine, I've been thinking about everything we learned during this trial, and it hit me that many of us suffer from hidden feelings."

"What do you mean?"

"It seems to me that everybody has some degree of hidden feelings—some try to bury them because we don't want to think about them or deal with them, and some don't show their feelings until they are forced to. Patricia had been holding on to her hidden feelings for years. She had been raped as a teenager and didn't tell anyone for over thirty years. I'm included in that, as well—look at all the hidden feelings that I never dealt with from a kid until now, not having a dad around to show me what a man is or how he is supposed to act and treat a woman and share what he is feeling with his woman."

"Yea, I guess you're right. Now you got me thinking about my own hidden feelings."

"As men and women, we need to take time out from time to time just to deal with our own hidden feelings. I mean, the more we do a self-evaluation, the better we can become."

"Wow, Troy—you might really be on to something; that right there will help some people."

"Another example would be for people who have been subjected to domestic violence; they are usually victims of domestic violence themselves. It becomes a vicious cycle that we need to break, and with you on the job, it can be done one family at a time."

"Thank you, I'm glad you have so much confidence in me. I'm nervous and anxious all at the same time."

"That's understandable; it's a whole new world you are about to dive into. Coming from the criminal side, handling big cases to civil cases, is a big change; however, if anyone can do it, you can. You know and understand the law, you're good with people, and most importantly you're compassionate and understand people—that alone puts you above most of these attorneys who only think of the money that they can make from the people."

As Troy and Jasmine continue to talk about the future of the new practice, Jasmine sees something move past the window that startles her. "Troy, did you see that?"

"See what? I didn't see anything."

"I could have sworn I saw someone looking in the window. It was in the corner of the window and when I looked up, I thought I saw them move away."

"Well, let me go check. Stay right here and I'll go look around and out back."

"Troy, be careful!"

"I will." Troy arms himself with a baseball bat and heads outside.

"I've looked around and I didn't see anyone, but I can't tell if anyone has been here. Maybe it was just a shadow or something passing by."

"No, Troy, I'm sure I saw someone looking in the window."

"I'm not saying I don't believe you, but when I went out there, I didn't see anyone, nor did I see any signs of anyone out there."

Suddenly, Troy's car alarm begins to go off. He runs to the window, looking all around and again he doesn't see anyone or anything that would have tripped his alarm. Troy goes back outside to search for anyone or any clues as to what may have set off the alarm—again, nothing. He heads back into the house.

"Troy, did you find anything or see anyone?" "No, I didn't see anything."

"Do you think it could be someone from the trial that didn't like the decision?"

"I don't think so, but I can't say for sure. I didn't notice anyone following me, and I went to the store before I came here. Did you check the camera on the doorbell?"

"Yes, I did, and I didn't see anything on there, either.

This is crazy."

"Has this ever happened before?" "No, not at all."

"Ok, well we need to put up some cameras on the outside just to be safe. Is that ok with you?"

"Yea, I guess so."

"If it makes you feel better, you and Tre could come and stay at my place for as long as you like."

"Thank you, but do you really think it's that serious?"

"I don't know, but I would rather be safe than sorry. How about you guys just come and stay for a couple of nights, at least until we get the camera's installed."

"Ok, let's get some stuff together and go to your place for a couple of days."

"Sounds good. I will call my handy man today and get him started right away. In the meantime, we can get you guys settled in."

SECOND CHANGES

"Well Jasmine, what do you think of the office space?"

"This is nice, I think my clients will love it, too. I especially like the space you guys have set aside for a quiet room, where women can come and have a safe place to think and plan their next moves."

"Great, I'm glad you like it. Karen and the rest of the staff put all of this together. The women who come through these doors will have a second chance at life and so will their families."

"This is perfect! Troy, Terrance, thank you both so much for this; I can't wait to start."

"No thanks needed; this is something that everyone will benefit from."

"Hello, excuse me. I'm looking for Mr. Terrance Mays or Mr. Troy Brooks."

"What can we do for you?"

"I heard you guys were looking for me…or should I say someone who has been sexually assaulted by Senator Johnson."

"Yea, we were looking for you because we needed some witnesses to help with our case. The trial is over now, though, and we won't be needing any witnesses."

"That's not why I'm here, though. I need your help."
"Ma'am, what can we do for you?"

"I need your help because not only was I assaulted, I have information on how the senator was getting young women like myself from Georgetown to come and intern for him, or even work for him. The senator wasn't the only one involved in this—there is a group of very powerful men trafficking young women out of that school, and a few others for their pleasure. Some are turned into high class prostitutes, some are used as mules for drug trafficking, and some have come up missing. These men are ruthless and unforgiving; they will do anything to keep their money, power, and status."

"How do you know all of this?"

"I used to be a part of that world. Like I said, I worked for the senator. He liked me, so I became his personal assistant. I kept records for him; I made certain arrangements for him for when he was in the mood; with certain young women, I arranged their meetings or hook ups. Once I got pregnant by him and was going to have his baby, so he sent me away so no one would know that we had a child together. I'm not from here and I don't have any family, so no one missed me. He didn't want me to make any friends, and he controlled my money—everything I had he controlled. Once I began to gain some weight from being pregnant, he wasn't attracted to me anymore and was done with me. He got me set up out of town with a place and he gave me some money. When I ran out of money, I had reached out to him and that's when I found out that he had died. Now me and my son are out here all alone; I have no job and I have been living out my car for the last three months with my five-year-old son."

"Did his wife know anything about all of this?"

"No, she had no clue who her husband really was— we made it look very legit to the outside world. All she knew was that I was one of his assistants; I would even go on trips with the senator and whenever he felt the urge, he would come to my room and have his way with me and then go back. We were very discreet about our entanglement; I kept my head down and did what I was told."

"Does anyone else know about this?"

"No, like I said, we were very discreet about it all. However, I did keep some incredibly detailed notes with dates, times, and names in my diary, just in case anything ever happened. A couple of weeks before the senator died, I had reached out to him for some money, and he told me that he was done with me and didn't want me to ever contact him again. Right after that, I started getting random phone calls and no one would say anything. I would see people looking in my windows, but when I went to see if someone was there, I could never find anyone, or my car alarm would all of a sudden just go off for no reason. I went to the police about it, but without any proof there was nothing that they could do. After that, I went into hiding. I'm scared and I don't know what to do. However, I do know that these men are very powerful and will do anything to keep their secrets. I need your help—I don't have anyone else I can turn to about this and I'm scared."

"You don't have to be afraid anymore. We got you!" Jasmine embraces the young women. "Ma'am, what is your name?"

"My name is Melody, but I go by Mel."

"Ok Mel, do you have your diary with you?" "Yes, I have it right here."

"May we look at it?"

"Yes, you can look at it." Mel hands the diary to Terrance.

"Mel, are you and your son still living in your car?" "Yes, we are; we don't have anywhere else to go."

"Well, we are going to put you up in a hotel until we can figure out what we are going to do next. Would that be ok?"

"Yes, that would be fine. Thank you very much; I appreciate it. Would it be possible for you to get me something to eat? I spent my last few dollars on gas last night to keep the car running for us to stay warm. I promise I'll pay you back."

"Yes, we can get you something to eat. Both of you can follow me and I'll take you to get something to eat. Jasmine, while you take her in the back, Terrance and I will be looking over this diary. We will be in my office. Follow me this way."

"What do you think, T?"

"Just from glancing over this, Troy, there are some major players in this diary. We not only have senators, but judges, lawyers, doctors, professional athletes, etc. This is like a whose list of names, and it's filled with dates, times, and detailed notes."

"What are we getting ourselves into here?"

"Troy, are you sure that you want to take this on? It could mean a lot of trouble for some very powerful people."

"I already know, bro." Jasmine walks into Troy's office.

"Well, what do you guys think? Is she telling us the truth?"

"According to her diary, she is. What do you think Jasmine?"

"I have my first client."

"Are you sure you want to tackle this case for your first one?"

"Oh yea, Mel desperately needs our help! Isn't this what we signed up for? To help the innocent and the ones who can't defend themselves?"

"Yea that's true. Well, let's get to work. We will follow your lead, Jasmine."

"Mr. Brooks, Marla Bordeaux is here to see you!"

ALSO, BY ROYCE DIXON SR.

HIDDEN FEELING REVEALED: THE SERIESAND MORE

HIDDEN FEELINGS

by Royce Dixon Sr.| Publication Date: December 2, 2018

HIDDEN FEELINGS REVEALED | IS THERE MORE
by Royce Dixon Sr. | Publication Date: June 18, 2023

BLESSED WHILE BROKEN
by Royce Dixon Sr. | Publication Date: January 2, 2020

JOJO'S LEARNING ADVENTURES
by Royce Dixon Sr. | Publication Date: February 15, 2021

ABOUT THE AUTHOR

ROYCE DIXON SR.

Royce Dixon Sr. is a passionate writer, photographer, and entrepreneur hailing from Rockford, IL. Born to Roy and Betty Dixon, Royce, Sr. grew up in a loving family alongside his siblings Karen and Delvin. He cherishes his family dearly and is a dedicated husband to Lisa Dixon and father to his children Tracina and Royce II, also known as TJ.

Royce, Sr. pursued his education at East High School in Rockford before furthering his studies and earning an Associate's degree in Business Administration from AIU Online College. During his academic journey, Royce, Sr. became a proud member of the esteemed Phi Beta Sigma fraternity, reflecting his commitment to excellence and personal growth.

Beyond his educational accomplishments, Royce, Sr. has embarked on various entrepreneurial endeavors. He is a co-owner of I Still Do Marriage Ministries, Be Blessed Clothing and Be Blessed Photography, showcasing his creative talents and eye for capturing special moments. Additionally, Royce Sr. is an accomplished author, having penned the books "Hidden Feelings," "Blessed While Broken," and "JoJo's

Learning Adventures." His written works delve into the depths of human emotions and experiences.

Driven by his passion for helping others, Royce Sr. finds joy in providing assistance to those in need. He dedicates his time to community service, actively participating in church activities and contributing to charitable causes.

Beyond his many accomplishments, Royce possesses a compassionate soul that is deeply affected by the plight of hurting and neglected children. Even commercials depicting their struggles evoke a profound sense of sadness within him, highlighting his empathetic and caring nature.

As Royce continues to explore new ventures, including this project "Hidden Feelings Revealed: Is There More," readers can anticipate more heartfelt and thought-provoking works from this multi-talented author. Through his endeavors and unwavering dedication, Royce Dixon, Sr. strives to touch lives, spread positivity, and make a lasting difference in the world.